ARE WE NOT MEN?

ARE WE NOT MEN?

Stories by

BRENT SPENCER

ARCADE PUBLISHING • NEW YORK

FIC
S745lar

FIRST EDITION

The characters and events in this book are fictitious. Any similarity to real persons, living or dead, is coincidental and not intended by the author.

Some of the stories in this collection were first published, though in slightly different form, in the following magazines: "All I Ever Wanted" (*Antioch Review*); "Babyman" (*The Missouri Review*); "Haven't You Ever Seen Cary Grant?" (*American Literary Review*); "The Hazards of Poetry" (*Stanford Magazine*); "The Small Things That Save Us" (*The Atlantic Monthly*); "This Is the Last of the Nice" (*GQ*).

Library of Congress Cataloging-in-Publication Data
Spencer, Brent.
    Are we not men? : stories / by Brent Spencer. —1st ed.
        p.   cm.
    ISBN 1-55970-357-1
    1. United States—Social life and customs—20th century—Fiction.
I. Title
PS3569.P4458A87 1996
813'.54—dc20   96–18979

Published in the United States by Arcade Publishing, Inc., New York
Distributed by Little, Brown and Company

10 9 8 7 6 5 4 3 2 1

BP

Designed by API

PRINTED IN THE UNITED STATES OF AMERICA

Rose

CONTENTS

I'm grateful for timely and generous support from the Nebraska Arts Council. And for the sharp eyes and keen sympathies of Leslee Becker, Tim Bent, Rose Catacalos, Peter Fish, Nadine Gordimer, Doris Grumbach, Fred Haefele, Donald Hall, Ehud Havazelet, John Hawkes, Jack Leggett, John L'Heureux, Lynne McFall, Tom McNeal, James Alan McPherson, Leonard Michaels, Bharati Mukherjee, Brad Owens, Nancy Packer, Gail Perez, and Phil Rizzo, and Ilena Silverman.

"What could it mean? A locked enclosure on a lonely island, a notorious vivisector, and these crippled and disoriented men?..."

—H. G. Wells, *The Island of Dr. Moreau*

ARE WE NOT MEN?

Are We Not Men?

*T*HE DEFINING MOMENT OF YOUR LIFE isn't even from your life. It's from the movies. But then, your whole life has never been more than a string of B-movie moments, so what's the difference? You know someone whose defining moment is in Terence Malick's *Days of Heaven*, when Brooke Adams loses the crystal goblet in the stream. For another it's Jack Nicholson in *Five Easy Pieces*, punching the roof, the steering wheel, the dash, shaking himself stupid.

For you the movie is Erle Kenton's 1932 classic, *Island of Lost Souls*. Charles Laughton plays H. G. Wells's mad doctor carrying out his forbidden experiments on the innocent animals of the island, turning them into beast-men. You saw it for the first time as a teenager, late one night after you discovered that your girlfriend, who sang folk songs and lit scented candles, and who therefore should have had more integrity, had never broken up with her old boyfriend. Perhaps this explains everything. Perhaps nothing. You watched, weeping, as the beast-men were forsaken by their creator and made strangers to themselves.

Charles Laughton introduces Richard Arlen to Lota, the Panther Woman. He wants them to mate, but he doesn't want to force it. He wants it to happen naturally, so to speak. As their eyes meet, he bounces the ends of his fingers together, his face glistening like fresh pastry. Their offspring will be the crowning achievement of his mad science, making up for all the whimpering, suppurating mistakes roaming the jungle and caged in his laboratory, his "House of Pain."

Time passes. You can't even remember the name of that folk-singing phony. Now you're married, but even this is no more real to you than a movie. You met in college, in art class, where your charcoal drawings were always smudged, where your abstract paintings were always too representational, and where your pots exploded in the kiln or came out like petrified bear scat.

For her final critique, your future wife presented a plaster head that might have been knocked off the shoulders of a Roman senator. When it was your turn, you wheeled in a wooden column on a hand truck. You'd stolen it from a demolition site — Corinthian, the top five feet, its shaft fluted, its capital carved with acanthus leaves and volutes. You'd used three tubes of airplane glue to stud the thing with broken wine bottles. As the class watched, you sprayed it with lighter fluid and set it on fire. Everyone clapped. Everyone cheered.

That night your future wife took you to dinner. She described your sculpture as "brilliant," a "self-consuming artifact." You talked for hours about fresco techniques, atonal music, whether photography is an art. Later you made love. Later still you got an A in art. What you never told her, told anyone, is that you had grown tired of the teacher pointing out the "lack of integrity in your line," the "listlessness of your brush stroke," that you'd given up on the class, that "Flaming Column with Wine Bottles" was meant as mockery.

In the jungle, Charles Laughton leads Bela Lugosi and the other beast-men in a pep rally:
"What is the Law?"
"Not to run on all fours! *That* is the law! Are we not Men?"
"What is the Law?"
"Not to eat meat! *That* is the law! Are we not Men?"
"What is the Law?"
"Not to spill blood! *That* is the law! Are we not Men?"

Marriage is expensive, you realize with bitterness, and a few lame notions about atonal music do not constitute a marketable skill. As part of your application for a job selling shoes at Sears, you're asked to take a personality test. In answer to one item — "To me, movies are more real than life" — you check the box under "Yes, definitely." They hire you anyway.

*   *   *

Now, at the end of four and a half years, all the pretty talk has run out. You and your wife have become bored with each other — with your puny opinions, with your daily routines, even with the moles on your backs. You're down to yourselves at last.

One night you go out for celluloid therapy, *Les Enfants du Paradis*. If there's anything left of the bond between you, this movie — the first you ever saw together — should reseal it. Back then, in the drafty basement of the old church, you sat holding each other long after the last credits had scrolled away, crying in the dark.

But this time is different. This time she says she can't think what she ever saw in it. When you say it's still the best movie ever made, she says, "A *mime*, for god's sake." You go home in silence, both knowing it isn't love unless you like the same movies.

The signs are clear. The orbit of your marriage is in decay. There's nothing left to do but make sure no innocent by-standers are harmed by your crash.

Night after night, you stand among your feral-faced brothers, hackles bristling, shuddering with self-pity, as Charles Laughton calls to you: "What is the Law?"

Why can't it be some other movie? Cary Grant in *Notorious*, Cary Grant in *Bringing Up Baby*, Cary Grant in anything? The trouble is, the only other movie that speaks to you is Richard Widmark's *Kiss of Death*.

*   *   *

4

Before you can raise the subject of divorce, your father-in-law dies. Your wife says his death has taught her that she's made all the big decisions of her life in an effort to please him. You, she says, were one of those decisions. Instead of feeling offended, you're relieved to find an excuse to end the marriage, one that lets you blame the dead instead of each other. But when she shows you a revised list of her priorities, you're oddly shaken to see that your name does not appear, not as costar, not as best boy, not even as gaffer.

You rent a cheap apartment in a bad neighborhood. All night the rats in the walls keep you awake with their gnawing. You furnish the place with a mattress, a split-seamed recliner, a cup, a spoon, a dish. You ride your bicycle twenty to thirty miles a day. You tell yourself you're getting in shape, but you ride until you can't walk, until you can do no more than stagger home through the rubble of broken auto glass and car stereo faceplates.

Still. Here no one expects anything of you. Here the phone won't ring, nor will the doorbell. Here you're safe, unloved and unloving, perfect and inviolate. You wonder if anyone has ever died from living on candy bars and brandy.

In the movie in your mind, the beast-men go to Paris for a much-deserved holiday. But they're ridiculed for their bad French, no one can get used to eating meals he hasn't had to chase down, and the natives are rude to the Dog Man.

*   *   *

5

Things are looking up. In a bar you meet a woman named Margaret who calls herself Summer and who says sex is all right but the idea of a real relationship is out, and are you OK with that?

For some it's a sound. The screen filled with whizzing arrows in Olivier's *Henry V.* The camels moaning awake in *Lawrence of Arabia.* The pounding hooves of Marlene Dietrich's army riding up the palace stairs in *The Scarlet Empress.*

Back in Paris, the Panther Woman feels right at home. She's tired of Richard Arlen's fear of commitment. She buys a designer original and prowls the streets, looking for Gerard Depardieu. The rest of the beast-men finish out their vacation in the *pension,* watching television.

"Ne sommes-nous pas des hommes?"

You're not OK with Summer. You don't like being with someone so uncommitted. The better the sex, the sadder you become. Why won't she love you, so you can start looking for a reason to leave her? At a party you flirt with other women, but she seems not to notice. Without warning, you stop seeing her, calling her. She seems not to notice.

Your ex-wife calls one day to say she's realized your divorce is the best thing that ever happened to her, and she hopes it's been good for you, too.

*   *   *

Face it, the beast-men will never go to Paris. You and your
brothers are doomed to roam the jungle outside the doctor's
compound, deformed by your desire to be something —
anything — else. You press your unbelieving hands against
your changing face. You don't know if it's loneliness you can't
stand or your own company. Somewhere a bird cries out.
Somewhere something dies.

Your ex-wife calls again, this time to see if you want to go out
for cioppino.

You say, "Not if you only want to tell me how happy
you are."

She says, "You must find a way to deal with your rage."

She drives. It feels as if someone's following you, but all
the cars and all the angry drivers look alike.

At dinner she suggests many ways to make yourself hap-
pier. She suggests books, she offers to introduce you to
women. "We're not really breaking up," she says, waving her
hand. "We're just entering a new stage of our relationship."

You can't help yourself. "Didn't you love me at all?"

"Of *course* I loved you," she says. "I *still* love you." She
covers your hand with hers. "It's be*cause* I love you that we're
doing this."

You slide your hand out from under hers. "Well, I don't
love you. In fact, I'd like to push you under a bus."

She leans back and smiles.

Your anger confuses you. Isn't this what you want? A fresh
start? But not like this. You want the Gary-Cooper-in-*High-*

Noon ending, the Clint-Eastwood-in-*Dirty-Harry* ending. You want to fling your star on the table and walk out with your head high.

She says, "That sense of humor — that's what'll pull you through this bad patch."

On the way home the streets are emptier and you see that it's true, you are being followed. When your ex-wife parks in front of your building, a car pulls in behind her. In the darkness you can see only a pale forehead, fingers tightly wrapped over the steering wheel.

Your ex-wife turns off the engine and says, "You don't *really* want to say good night to me, do you?"

As you walk with her to the door, you feel the eyes of Margaret/Summer burning into your back.

Inside, your ex-wife wants you to chase her around the apartment. You trap her in a corner, tugging at her clothes, muttering theatrical threats. Wait, she says, baring her breasts, wait, wait, wait.

Outside, a long angry howl splits the night. Summer is leaning on the horn. She leans on it for a long time. She leans on it until the howl is no more than a dry metallic ache.

Richard Arlen is interested in the Panther Woman despite himself. Perhaps it's her almond eyes, her hooked fingernails, the fact that she can outrun his Packard.

A few days later Margaret/Summer appears drunk at your door. "I have something to say," she says, but instead she just slaps you, twice, hard. At the second slap, your glasses fly into

8

the wall next to the bathroom door, one lens popping out. You both freeze, staring. A moment straight from the movies. Together you break into reckless laughter.

"Oh hell," she says, "we're such fools. I miss you. Let's take a chance on this love thing." You shake your head. You walk her slowly to the door, closing it softly after her. Somewhere, you hope, a camera's rolling.

Your ex-wife leaves a message on your machine, inviting you to the movies. You wait for her under the jolly marquee lights. She's late. Couples come and go. You gaze across the parking lot. You check your watch. The crowd trails inside.

Later, another message on your machine: she's changed her mind, she's sorry, she's afraid going out again might give you the wrong idea. "Our project right now," she says, "is to move forward, not backward."

In your dreams you no longer see the tender, mangled faces of your brothers gazing up at the doctor's House of Pain. Instead, you see a shining surgery all around you, rows of glass beakers filled with smoky chemicals, trays of stainless-steel instruments. Bela's dark whisper is far away: "Are we not Men?" You're not sure anymore. Are you the lonely beast-man or the doctor with the scalpel eyes?

Weeks pass, and then months. There is no new woman. In fact, women look at you with suspicion, even the ones who don't know you. You've developed a reputation. You wish they'd describe you as "dangerous," but the words they use are "fucked up."

As a kid, you were always good at hide-and-seek. Too good. You found the best hiding places — lying quietly on a flat-topped garage, crouching inside a loaded dumpster, slipping into the cellar of a stranger's house. You hid so well that your friends finally gave up and went home, leaving you out there hiding from nothing, from no one.

It's late. You're watching the movie again, this time with the sound off. The end is coming, when the beast-men rise up and carry their maker into his own laboratory. But not yet, not yet. Your phone rings. A woman whose voice you don't recognize says, "I just want to know why." You pull the phone out by its root.

Hollywood movies make you sick. The new ones. They're always about men, real bastards, who wake up from life-threatening illnesses as nicer people. Men who become wildly generous and compassionate, who right every wrong they've ever committed, who are forgiven, even by their enemies. Hollywood once knew that the opposite is true, that behind every polite smile is a raging, lunatic, cannibal, alien ax murderer.

When you close your eyes, you can't see your wife's face or the face of any woman you've ever known. Instead, you see your sculpture in flames. Wine labels blackening in the heat, smoke funneling from the broken bottle necks. You're not a beast. You're not a man. You're not even the mad doctor. You've become your sculpture, a self-consuming artifact.

This time, near the end of the movie, you finish a gallon of Scotch, a leftover from your wedding reception and all that remains of your marriage.

Richard Arlen and the Panther Woman race through the jungle to safety. The doctor's compound is in flames. A beast-man lumbers after them, but Lota leaps on him catlike from a paleolithic tree. It will do no good. It never does. But this time — before she can die in your arms, gazing up into your eyes and saying, "Go . . . go back . . . sea" — this time, you cry out "No!" and pitch the empty Scotch bottle into the beast-man's surprised face.

All that was long ago. Now you live in a quiet town where the dairy still delivers. You don't miss television. In the evenings you read Trollope to each other or listen to Bach. Who'd have guessed that the Panther Woman had a domestic side? That she'd have talents for Thai food and cabinetry?

It seems as though you've lived together forever. You love her long limbs, her dark tangled hair, her pale gray eyes, green in the right light. Some nights, it's true, you find her standing at an open window, alert to every trace of sound and scent, the stubborn beast flesh creeping back. But mostly, she says, she doesn't miss the old days, not even Gerard Depardieu, who turned out to be something of a brute.

At last you love your life.

Babyman

I DID TIME AT FAIRHOPE MEN'S CORRECTIONAL Facility in Pennsylvania. Not hard time. Time. I thought wanting something bad enough was all it took. I thought a move or two would put me in the clear, where no one could touch me. I was young and stupid and I didn't know anything, but by the time I realized that, it was too late.

Three weeks into my sentence, Ronnie came to see me. She was the only person I put on my list of approved visitors. After "Relationship" I wrote "Wife." Even though we never made it legal, I figured four years had to count for something. In the beginning we spent all our time in bed, out of breath, blood pounding, just drank each other up. But near the end we took turns trying to kill each other, slow secret killing, the kind of crime only married people can commit.

She was sitting halfway down the long table in the visitors' room, her hands clapped over one of the clear plastic purses they make women visitors use.

As I crossed the room, my mind went back to our first

night. We met on the dance floor at a bar called The Hourglass. Later she took me to her place. She made me turn out
the light before she'd take her clothes off, but I flipped it back
on and saw this naked woman lifting the top of her head off.
She was wearing a fall, a big horse tail of brown hair. Remembering that night made me laugh.

"What's so funny?" she said, eyes flashing, always ready
for the fight.

"Nothing," I said. "I'm just glad to see you." Her hair was
longer now, and she was letting the blond grow out. I forgot
how much like a kid she looked. One of her front teeth was
crooked and crossed behind the one next to it a little. When
she was nervous, she'd slide her tongue over it. She was doing
that now.

The stall on our right was empty. On the other side, an old
black woman was crying because she spent all week cooking for
her grandson and now they wouldn't let her bring the food in to
him. The kid kept saying, "It's OK, Grammy. It's OK," but you
could tell he was missing that fried chicken and pecan pie.

Ronnie asked me how was I and were they treating me
OK and all like that. Small talk. But that ran out long before
our time was up. We just sat there staring at each other over
the glass partition, listening to that old woman. "Meat loaf
with lots of onions and pickle relish in it and German potato
salad and a whole big bag of butter cookies. . . ."

Ronnie was chewing the side of her fingernail, where the
skin was already torn and sore-looking, but now she forced
herself to put her hands back on the purse. "Ray," she said. Her
voice was a tight whisper. "When we were together, you know,

just before they put you away . . . well, I'm sorry, but it looks like you got me pregnant."

". . . a dozen deviled eggs and a jar of them black olives you like, the ones with. . . ."

"Ronnie," I said.

She looked down at her hands, and her hair fell across her face. She was talking faster now. "I know what I need to do, but it costs money, you know?"

My heart was climbing up my throat. A baby.

She looked up then, looked straight at me. "Five hundred dollars is what I need."

I said, "Honey, are you sure you —"

"Listen," she said, standing up quickly, "if you don't want to help me, just say so. I don't even want to *be* here."

I reached over the partition and held the ends of her fingers. Her eyes went away when I did that. I said, "I'm sorry, honey. I don't know what to say. I'll get you the money. Don't worry."

At the end of the room, the guard stepped out his cigarette and hiked up his pants. He started down the long table. When he was standing behind me, he said, "All done." I let go of Ronnie's hands. She pulled them away and held them to her chest like hurt things.

I hated prison, hated everything about it. Hated living two to a cell the size of a parking space. Hated the nickel-and-dime hustlers, the pain experts, the state hospital rejects. I hated the food, the weather, and the warden. I hated the hacks — the hardasses who hit you where it wouldn't show and the do-gooders who had you begging for brutality just to keep

15

your self-respect. I hated shakedowns and lockdowns and the rotten smell of men in hot weather.

The prison was noisy that night — cell doors slamming, men yelling. My cellmate, an old guy, bald except for a bit of gray fluff at the back of his head, wouldn't turn off his radio until way late. Frank liked all that crying and dying hillbilly crap. He was easy enough to get along with, except for that. He'd stare at the radio while he listened. What'd he think — he'd see the lips moving? I could usually tune it out, but this time I couldn't sleep. I was sick about Ronnie. I wrote a letter to Eddie Kaczmarek, a friend of mine in the money business. I never hated prison so much as I hated it that night.

The next morning, I woke up exhausted, in no mood for work. Frank and I were the prison meat processors — checking in the new men. Fingerprints, photos, case records, medical cards, property cards, personal profiles. Frank ran the place. He'd been in Fairhope so long everybody thought of him as one of the staff.

Nothing went right that day. In the middle of processing a busload of new inmates, the *e* on my typewriter died. The phone never worked very well, but now I had to drop it on the floor to get a dial tone. And while I was shooting ID photos, the damn camera froze up on me.

Frank showed me a drawer full of pictures — half profiles, half full-face — all of the same guy. "Put two of these in his folder." Until they fixed the camera, everybody we took in would be white, bald, over forty, and have a harelip.

That worked until the last man came through. The last man was Louis Conrad. When I called his name, he stood up so fast his chair banged against the baseboard heater. He had a washed-out face and thin, reddish-brown hair. His big mustache almost covered his mouth. He sat down in the chair next to my desk and lowered his eyes, fingering his mustache. Fresh meat. Just up from County. A man used to waiting, to being pushed around. He didn't breathe, he sighed.

But when he saw the fake pictures going into his file, he cleared his throat and said, "That ain't me."

I gave him a look and said, "I know. It doesn't matter. Just sign the forms."

"It matters to me." He straightened the papers lying on the desk beside him. His hands were shaking. "I won't sign nothing with my wrong face on it."

I said, "The camera's busted. Don't give me a hard time."

He looked up at the ceiling and sucked in his lower lip. He smoothed his mustache like he was petting a cat. When he looked down, his eyes were wet.

He said, "I work nights. Used to work. The weaving mill over in Scranton. In the two years I had that job I never got used to the hours."

I held the pen out to him. "I can't hear this. You can't go telling me this."

He said, "I got home one day. I was so tired. I just wanted to rest, put my head down for a while. But the baby started crying. I had to get some sleep. She was crying so loud. I only wanted her to stop crying."

I laid the pen down carefully, like it was about to go off.

"And the point is . . ." He was staring at the floor. He

17

shook his head. He looked up and touched the file folder. "I want it all in there. And I want my right face."

Frank was in the john. I unclipped the fake pictures. I said, "We can do this later, when the camera's fixed."

I sent him to Supply for prison blues and bedding. As quiet as I could, I banged the phone against the desk until I got a tone. Then I dialed Ronnie's number. If they caught me, they'd take my job away and send me to DW, Detention Wing.

As soon as she picked up, I said, "I need to know why you don't want to have the baby."

"What? Who is this?" She sounded mad but a little curious.

"It's because I'm in prison, isn't it," I said. "You're ashamed of me. I can understand that. Things are pretty bad between us."

She knew who it was now, and in a hard, flat voice she said, "You don't want to send the money. Is that what this is about?"

I said, "If money's what you want, you'll have it inside a week. Just say the word. But I think we could be making a mistake" — talking loud now, talking fast — "I think we could be making a big mistake. A baby might turn things around for us. Think of it. We could be all right with a kid, don't you know?"

She sounded small and worn out. "Forget about it, Ray."

"Forget what?"

"Everything. Just forget about everything."

I heard Frank flush the toilet. I said, "I can't, Ronnie. I

can't. I'll call you later." I hung up just as he was coming out. It wasn't something he'd want to know about.

Almost every day after that I called her, working on her, trying to get her to see things my way.

"At least tell me you'll think about it."

"OK."

"OK you'll have the baby or OK you'll think about it?"

"Goodbye, Ray."

After a while, she wouldn't even answer the phone, but I swore I could feel her sitting next to it, watching it ring, thinking. I told Frank I had to catch up on my filing, and he got me permission from the associate warden to go to the office after supper one night. She picked up right away.

"Don't hang up," I said. "Don't say anything. Just hear me out." She was still on the line, so I kept talking. "In here they say, 'Today is the first day of the rest of your life.' They think that's some kind of answer, but it's the whole fucking problem."

"You're the problem, Ray," she said, real quiet, real firm. "It was always only you."

"I know that," I said, but she got to me. She always could.

She had me thinking about the time I broke all the windows of our Impala with a baseball bat. She wasn't in it or anything. Still, a bad time.

"So what are you saying?"

"I'm saying I'm not going to be in here forever. What am I going to do with the rest of my life? I don't want to spend it doping and drinking, some kind of police character. That's so lame. I think a kid could help me keep my head clear."

She was quiet for so long I thought she walked away from the phone. Then she said, "That's a lousy reason to have a kid."

"But there's worse reasons," I said. "Lots worse."

At first she didn't say anything. Then she said, "What difference would that make, a baby?"

"It'd make a difference to me." Before she could say anything back, I said, "Maybe it's the only thing that will. And besides, there's stuff we could teach a kid, stuff nobody but us knows."

She was still quiet, but I knew she was there. I could hear her breathing. Her dad was a hitter and mine was a drunk. We used to talk about having a kid and raising it right. I thought she might be thinking of that now. She didn't say anything for the longest time, and when she did, her words came out slow and careful, like bad news. "OK, Ray. All right."

"You'll have the baby?"

It was more like a short, sharp breath than a word. "Yeah."

"If you're nervous about money," I said, "don't be. Money's not a problem." I touched my shirt pocket, where I was still carrying the letter to Kaczmarek. "I can get money. All you want."

"Ray —"

"I mean it. That baby's going to get born in style." I said, "Six years will fly by like nothing. As soon as I'm out, we'll get married for real." My face was hot and my eyes burned. In six years, the baby wouldn't be a baby anymore.

She said, "I have to go, Ray," and there was nothing but dry wind crackling on the other end of the line.

I dug out my letter to Kaczmarek, changed the five hundred to five thousand, and slipped it in with the outgoing mail. Eddie had a reputation as a knee-breaker, but it was my kid, man. I was little again and she was Christmas.

In the next few weeks, I called Ronnie every time Frank's back was turned, but she was always too tired to talk. I wrote to her, letters full of questions. I wanted to know about every ache, every weird hunger.

She'd write back sometimes, mostly about the morning sickness, how some days she couldn't even get out of bed. Her letters didn't tell me much, though, so I filled in the gaps myself. When I wasn't processing inmates, I was talking babies, reading books about babies, writing away for information about babies. I was a nut on the subject. I even traced pictures from a medical book so I could keep track of what the baby looked like in the womb.

I started sending Ronnie tips from all the books and magazines I was reading. The mattress should fit into the crib snugly and the slats should be no more than two and a half inches apart, for safety. Hang a mobile over the crib and paint a bull's-eye at one end, because babies like colors and shapes.

Late at night I'd lie awake, talking to the baby in my mind. I'd tell her all about myself. I'd tell her where I went wrong. I'd tell her the things I could change and the things I couldn't. I'd fall asleep thinking maybe she could hear me and maybe she was thinking of me, too. Right then. Right that very second.

Ronnie was nine days overdue. I skipped breakfast and snuck into the office before eight to call her. They could give me three days in the "quiet box" for that.

She said, "How would *you* know the baby's late?"

"Because I'm keeping a chart," I said. "I have it all timed out."

"Everything's fine, Ray. Don't worry." That's what she said, but she sounded worried to me.

Two weeks later, sitting around the cell, I got a letter from Ronnie. When I opened it, a little picture fell into my lap. It was of a squirmy-looking baby with a lick of black hair like mine. Her face was all snarled up and red, and she was staring straight at me.

Frank was lying in the top bunk with his radio balanced on his stomach. I held the picture up for him to see. He smiled and said, "I don't see no baby in that picture." He cocked his hand over his eyes like he was trying to see something far away. He said, "I'm looking, but all I see is a lumpy little blanket."

"Look again," I said, snapping the picture in his face. "That's my kid, man."

He slipped on his reading glasses and took the picture from me, held it close. "This little bitty thing with the mashed-up face?"

"Yeah."

"This is a baby?"

"Elizabeth," I said. Elizabeth.

Ronnie and I worked out a plan. Once a month she'd park down on the county road and tap the horn three times. I wouldn't let them come inside. I didn't want my kid's first memory to be the slam of a cell door. When I'd look out between the bars, she'd be standing beside the car, holding Elizabeth high up over her head, trying to keep her face away from the kicking feet. That's how I watched my kid get bigger, from a quarter mile away, through a ten-foot wall of chain link and razor wire. To me that coiled wire looked like angel hair.

Elizabeth changed everything. I even started to like my job. The fingerprints I took were so good you could hang them in a museum. On the forms, I'd fill in every little space, right down to "Religious Preference." I can spell "Rastafarian" now because of that job. I made a sign to inspire the new meat. Now, when I took their pictures, they were staring straight at The Convict's Prayer. DEAR LORD, FORGIVE ME MY WRONGS IN THE DAYS OF MY LOW LIVING AND LEAD ME ON THE PATH OF BLAH BLAH BLAH. You should see the deep looks I caught.

Ronnie sent more pictures, I sent more money. I showed Elizabeth to everybody. I was crazy about her, right? She looked like a little gangster, except for the slicked-up curl on top of her head. I laughed every time I looked at it.

Pretty soon, guys started coming to me with questions.

On the yard, on the line, in the dining room, in the showers.

"Babyman, my two-year-old gets soap in his eyes every time the wife gives him a bath."

"Get him swimming goggles."

"Yo, Babyman, how come when my brother's kid spits up, the goop shoots clear across the room? They think she's possessed. Like the devil-girl in that movie."

"That's projectile vomiting. Tell him to get used to it."

I was getting a reputation. If I didn't know the answer right off, I looked it up. If I couldn't find it there, I used a little common sense. The prison library started ordering things for me — Dr. Spock's *Baby and Child Care, The Magic Years, Between Parent and Child.* I'm sure I'm the only guy in the whole prison system who ever subscribed to *Mothers' World.*

"Babyman, the wife says our kid won't sleep without whamming his head against the side of his crib. He's at it all the time — wham, wham, wham. She's afraid he'll knock himself stupid."

"Tell her to start the washing machine at bedtime and set him in a car seat on top. He'll be asleep by the rinse cycle."

Day and night I was talking babies, reading up about babies, dreaming about babies. Every time I talked to some guy about his kid, it was like talking about Elizabeth. I was the Babyman of Fairhope, and I didn't care who knew it.

By the end of two years, the baby business was going crazy. Every week I'd get a batch of letters from inmates' wives full of questions and advice. I started mailing out a newsletter I printed up on an old Ditto machine in Admin. I'd put in all the letters I was getting and add a comment sometimes underneath. My biggest issue was on how to stop thumb sucking. Six pages, front and back. People said cayenne pepper and Chinese mustard. They said jalapeño juice and a big gauze bandage. In my comment I said, "Maybe you could just leave the kid alone?"

Out of nowhere, in the middle of everything, I made parole. All the while I was passing out baby tips, the warden and the Bureau of Prisons were marking it down as "meritorious good time." I was so happy I howled. Nothing could touch that high. Hello my honey, hello my baby, hello good times, hello.

I should've had a friend pick me up, but I didn't have friends like that. I could've sent word to Ronnie, but I wanted to surprise her.

When they opened the gate, I walked down the hill, straight to the spot where Ronnie would stand with the baby. It was easy to find. Her old cigarette butts were scattered all over the ground. The prison was a big hateful-looking mother, four stories of granite and iron. I stared up at my cell. It's a funny thing. Standing there like that, I thought I could tell what it was like to be Ronnie. All she ever wanted from me was a made-up mind. Why was that too much to give?

The road ran between empty winter fields. Nothing but cold gray sunlight, rotting fences, and broken cornstalks. After a while, the woods closed in on both sides. I stopped walking when I saw an old Maverick parked in a stand of pines. It was puke green inside and out, the fenders and hood eaten up with rust. Hidden back among the trees was a little hunting shack all shut up tight, boards nailed over the doors and windows.

I stood next to the car, thinking how a whole month might go by before that old boy missed his beater. I found a big flat rock and broke the window on the driver's side.

The exhaust smelled like rotten eggs, and the car bucked every time I took it over forty. But I wasn't worried. I felt lucky. They could probably put a bullet in the engine and the son-of-a-bitch would still run.

When I got to town, it was already getting late. I picked up a bottle of Beam for courage, a six-pack for Ronnie and me, and some presents for Elizabeth — a Spider-Man comic book and a teething ring with red stars floating inside. I knew the presents were all wrong. Elizabeth was almost two by then, but that was all they had for kids at the Buy 'n' Fly.

The lights were on in Ronnie's house, in the living room and the front bedroom. I parked across the street and took a healthy hit of Beam. I folded my wallet open to Elizabeth's picture and propped it on the dash. It was one of the last ones Ronnie'd sent. A dime-store quickie, a washed-out shot of Elizabeth sitting by herself. She's looking up off the edge of the picture at someone standing in the doorway of the booth. She's got that what-am-I-doing-here look on her face. I know it well.

I guess I thought it would be easy, but now I was nervous. Altogether, three years had passed us right by. We'd be nothing but a houseful of strangers. Three years. So long I couldn't remember anymore what it felt like to be inside Ronnie, or the look of her face in the dark. What I remembered most was a few times late at night, after we were finished. She'd be lying there with her head on my arm, the air turning cold and me half dead and drifting off. Sometimes then she'd say things to me, whisper them. Things she'd never tell me any other time. She'd say, "I wish I was more beautiful for you," and once, "I'm afraid to die, Ray."

I walked right in like I was only gone to the corner store. Ronnie was lying on the couch in her robe, reading a magazine and smoking, her hair all over her head. The TV was on, with the sound low. Everything looked the same except for that TV. It was the size of a small car.

I said, "Hey."

She looked up, real shocked. "What are you doing here?"

"Surprise, surprise." I popped a beer and held it out.

She sat up and pulled her robe tight. "You're not supposed to be here." She didn't take the beer.

"Now don't get your blood in a flood. I didn't break out. They paroled me. Where's the baby? Asleep?"

She didn't answer. She just sat there chewing on the inside of her cheek and strangling her magazine.

I heard heavy footsteps coming downstairs, hands sliding along the walls. Ronnie turned to the doorway, looking boxed in. I felt my face go hard. I said, "That baby sure has grown."

When the guy dropped into the living room, he jerked up short like he just stepped in something. He was a scrawny

27

dude in a T-shirt and jeans. He had little, pinched-together eyes and stringy brown hair trailing out from under a Phillies cap. He turned to Ronnie and said, "It's him, isn't it."

I looked him up and down, slow, so he would feel my eyes on him. I took a deep pull of the beer I had opened and said, "You damn well better believe it's me. I suppose you're going to tell me you're the plumber."

His eyes flickered over me. "I ain't going to tell you jack shit, man." He laughed through his nose, a sneery laugh. In the old days I would have dropped him then and there, but the old days were gone.

I turned back to Ronnie. "Elizabeth upstairs?"

"Elizabeth," she said, like she didn't know her own daughter's name.

If I could see the baby, I figured, then everything would be all right. Then I'd know what to do. "Ronnie," I said, "just tell me where she is."

The guy's voice went quiet. He had this sick smile. He said, "You think you're so smart?"

I turned on him real cold. "*I* will tell you when to talk, my friend." I said, "Ronnie, other things might change" — I splashed a little beer at him — "but that's not going to change. There's still the baby between us."

Slowly, enjoying it, the guy said, "No there ain't."

Ronnie stood up and said, "Andy, stop."

He said, "Stay out of this, Veronica." He had his hand up like he was some kind of traffic cop.

"Stay out of it?" she said. "You didn't want me staying out of it when it was money you were after."

"I said stay out of it." He took a half-step toward her, and his hand turned into a fist.

Ronnie ignored him, but she was crying now. "It got all out of hand, Ray. I know it got way out of hand. But you made it worse than it had to be. You did. You wouldn't let it go."

I just stood there waiting for what they were telling me to sink in. It was like a rock falling down a deep well, and I was just waiting for it to hit bottom. From where I stood, I could see the neighbor's yard. It was full of toys — a Big Wheel, a tricycle, two skateboards, a hula hoop.

"It was the only thing we could come up with," Ronnie said quickly, wiping her face with the back of her hand. "I borrowed the baby from Andy's sister."

I looked around the room as if I could find something to prove she was lying — a rattle, a pile of dirty diapers, any of the things I sent her money to buy. There was nothing but the couch, the coffee table, a chair full of old magazines, and that monster TV. On the screen a woman was pulling a man down on a white rug in front of a fireplace. There was a lot of hair and heavy breathing, but to me they looked like a couple of corpses.

Andy must have thought I was about to make a move. He crouched a little, waving his fists at me. He said, "Come on, come on. Hit me, you fuck."

Ronnie held herself like she was cold. "It started with a pool bet," she said. "Big man here thinks he's got such a hot stick. I hate to tell you, but I could beat you one-handed."

BABYMAN

Andy took another half-step toward her. "I warned you, bitch."

I looked at him, then at her. I shook my head. I said, "Ronnie, Ronnie, what a sorry piece of shit you hooked up with."

His right hand caught me just under the eye. I dropped the six-pack and the presents and shoved him across the room. I pinned his neck to the wall with my elbow. I jacked him up off his feet a little. His eyes bugged out. His mouth went wide. The corners were shiny with spit.

Ronnie started beating on my back. She was crying and yelling at the same time. "Stupid, stupid, stupid."

Andy was breathing through his teeth now. I put my fist just under his chest and pushed, slow and hard. Every breath he took was shorter than the last. I wanted to hurt him bad. I wanted to step into his world.

But then I thought of what Ronnie used to say every time her period came. No babies this month. My eyes burned and my throat was tight. No babies this month. For a long second I couldn't feel anything but the kicking of his heart.

I let him go. He doubled over and dropped to his knees, rubbing his neck, wheezing and coughing.

I ran upstairs to see for myself. I couldn't help it. The back bedroom, where I always pictured Elizabeth surrounded by mobiles and bright colors, had the same old sofa bed I slept on so many times. The same black wire nightstand. The same fake-oak chest of drawers. Nothing else. Everything was the same in the front bedroom, too, except

30

there was a big new bed. The sheets were all balled up and the air smelled sour.

When I got back to the living room, Ronnie was kneeling next to Andy, holding his head to her chest, petting his stringy hair. Her eyes looked dead. She said, "I'm sick, Ray. Sick of everything. I'm sick of you and I'm sick of him, and I wish to God I never met the both of you." Her voice was wet and shaking. She said, "You'll get your money back. Just leave us alone."

"It's not the money," I said. "It's not the fucking money." I nodded at the guy. "It's not even this two-for-a-nickel, off-the-wall bullshit."

Andy sat up some, rubbing his neck. His voice was raw. All the toughness had gone out of him. He said, "You *threw* that money at us, man. We couldn't let it go. Besides, we were going to make it right with you."

I said, "You were going to make it *right* with me? How the fuck were you going to do that?" Ronnie sat back on the floor and stared at the comic book and the teething ring lying between us. They looked far away. Everything looked far away. "It's like you killed Elizabeth," I said. "It's just like you killed her."

"Elizabeth," Andy croaked. "That ain't even her real name."

I didn't know what to say. I was afraid of what would happen when the rock hit the bottom of the well. I took one last look at Ronnie and walked out of the house. I was halfway across the street when she came to the door. "You son-of-a-bitch!" she yelled. "You act like we were some kind of *love* birds!"

I ran back to the house, up on the porch, but she slammed the door in my face. I could feel her leaning against it. I said, "You could have told me a hundred other lies that would have worked, Ronnie. You didn't have to tell me this."

She was crying really something. She said, "I never loved you." Like that was supposed to explain everything.

I kicked the lawn chairs off the porch. I ripped a bush out of the ground and threw it at the door. I was afraid of what else I might do, so I went back to the car and got in. I slammed the door. I opened it and slammed it again, louder.

A black Trans Am was parked under the streetlight in front of the house, flames painted on the hood and fenders. I started the Maverick and pulled away from the curb, a little past the car. I stopped.

I guess in the back of my brain I always knew there was no baby. But if you believe in something hard enough, it's supposed to come true, isn't it? I knew the smell of her skin. I knew the curl of her hand. I knew the feel of her in my arms when she was hot from crying.

The Trans Am looked like it had just been washed. I leaned on my horn and kept leaning on it as Andy came out with the rest of my six-pack. I was still leaning on it as I threw the car in reverse and swung it back, slamming the Trans Am. He came off the porch at a run, screaming.

I pulled fifteen or twenty feet away, gunned the engine, then slammed it again. His windshield popped and the door fell off as I pulled away. Lights came on up and down the street. He danced around my car and grabbed at me through the broken window. I pulled farther off, giving myself a healthy run for one last shot. A beer can landed on my hood, exploding like a grenade. He ran back into the house. I slapped the car into reverse. I held the brake hard and hit the gas. The car shook, the tires screeched, and then I let it go.

It was beautiful. The whole left side of the Trans Am caved in. Glass and metal flew everywhere. One of the bucket seats jumped right out onto the sidewalk. I couldn't have done better with dynamite.

I drove off easy. In the mirror, I could see Andy come running back into the street with a pistol. He dropped into a crouch and squeezed off a wild shot. I slowed down some, just to fruit him. He ran a few yards, stopped, and fired again. He came zigzagging up the street like he had old war movies rolling through his head. The last round hit the back window with a flat slap that blew bits of glass into my hair. I figured that was close enough.

Three blocks down Westfall Boulevard, my muffler fell off and the engine started to hammer, but I was right about that car. It just wouldn't quit. From somewhere far away I heard a siren, so I hauled ass. Past the bars and the quick-stops and the fast-food places and the Trip-L-X Drive-In. I ran all out. I really floored it. Past the mall and the auto graveyard and the county landfill. I by God *drove.* Until the siren faded away. Until the city lights were long gone. Until there was nothing between me and Elizabeth but the road and the rising moon.

Save or Turn to Stone

"*Y*OU SHOULD HAVE VISITED LAST WEEKEND," she says as we stare at the icy sludge lying in the center of the green, all that's left of Winter Carnival. "The theme this year was 'Camelot Frozen in Time.' " Slushy castle walls drip in the February sun. Knights on horseback collapse onto stiff gray grass. Nearby, a man is chanting, "Change, change, change, change." I can't tell if he's a beggar or an evangelist.

It's Friday and happy hour in this New England college town. Anne's taking me for a drink to get a feel for the place, a method we've used on other towns.

The bars are filled with lacquered wood, beveled mirrors, and men in suits. It's been six months since she started teaching here, since we've seen each other. We talk about my job interview at a prep school in Massachusetts.

"It went well, I think."

"So what are you worried about?"

"I don't know. The cabdriver who took me to the interview said, 'I hope you like snotty little rich kids.' And besides teaching, I'd have to live in a dorm. I'd also have to coach a sport called Survival 101."

"You're kidding."

"No," I say. "You take kids into the woods and try to live off the land for days at a time."

"You?" she says. "You couldn't find your way out of a well-lit closet."

She's right and I laugh. I remember being lost along the Lehigh River. I was thirteen, a Scout at Camp Acahela. For hours I thrashed around in the woods. I thought the night would come and I would die, but then I saw a tent through the trees. Mine. I limped into the clearing, exhausted, covered with scratches, my ankle swollen and blue from a fall. At camp, everything was normal. My friends were swimming, carving wood, tying intricate knots in pieces of cord. I don't know what I expected. Search parties, I guess, helicopter reconnaissance. But no one noticed I was missing. No one knew that, purely by chance, I was still alive. I went to my tent and wept because I was lost in the woods and no one cared, and because I was too ashamed to tell anyone.

"You'll be fine," Anne says. "You'll get the job. I don't see what you're worried about."

"I'm worried I'll get the job."

We finish the night at a place called The Inn, where the waitress grudgingly brings another round after last call. And still we're able to get out before the bar lights go up.

In the street Anne says, "Well, we didn't find it." She means we didn't find the Truth, the epiphany that proves the world is worth the trouble.

"Don't despair."

"Despair I can handle," she says. "It's hope that kills."

Saturday we hold our heads in our hands and make sorrowful noises. We lie quietly on the rug for hours, thinking, listening to music — Kristofferson, Bach, it doesn't matter.

We lie in each other's arms and say, "We can't do this anymore." We mean drinking. Later we'll walk into town and browse the shops, eat dinner, and get an early start on another night of drinking.

She's tall and thin, an ex-athlete, ex-cheerleader, and there are parts of her life she no longer understands. Another person seems to have lived that life. Now she teaches philosophy. She's against shoddy thinking. "That's just bad philosophy," she'll say when she disagrees with me.

Her son, Tbor, is the Grandfather of Assassins. All he wants to talk about is the on-line game he plays with people he's never met. His cell leader, Mawa the Unmerciful, has it in for him.

"He was trying to get me killed by giving all these powers to Aldebaran — psionics, flame hurling, stuff like that." He's sprawled on a brown recliner, his voice quiet and careful.

"In the end, I had to die, but Mawa let me choose my death, so I turned into a ring of binding and made myself a gift to Aldebaran. When he put the ring on his finger, he got trapped in eternity. So in a way I guess I won." Anne and I laugh. We have both been married and divorced. We know about the ring of binding.

Tbor has been shuttling between parents for years. For the last two or three months he's lived with Anne.

"It must be hard to be moving all the time," I say.

"I'm used to it," he says quietly, the same careful tone he uses to tell his gaming adventures.

On Saturday afternoon, Anne and I go for a walk, leaving Tbor to his game. We call out goodbye, but the only answer is the sound of the keyboard's chatter and jab.

"I like him," she says, clapping her hands and cocking her head. "Isn't that amazing?"

The day is warmer than we thought, so we leave our gloves and scarves in a bookstore locker downtown. The streets are full of parents and children. Every shop is a wood-frame house with shutters, varnished floors, and hanging plants. Only the hardware store suggests that people need more to live their lives than homemade ice cream, running shoes, and two-for-one margaritas.

"What are we doing here?" she says with mock misery. She means why aren't we somewhere with real people and good bars and Okie music. She means how have our lives come down to this. I don't tell her that I envy her job and would trade places in a minute. But she knows.

"You buy all this, don't you," she says, gesturing at the crowded street.

"No," I say.

"Yeah?"

"A little." She has an office with enough bookshelves, an easy chair, and a window overlooking the green. I buy all of it.

"They're the same snotty kids you're so worried about teaching, only older, with more attitude. Were we ever like that?"

Lately, she says, she's been having strong flashbacks to her childhood. What it felt like walking to school. Practicing the piano for hours. Other times, too. Sitting beside a pool, drunk on rum and California sunshine.

I think I know what she means. The trouble is, too many things keep happening. Especially in memory, where everything happens at once. You're walking to grade school in Indiana, the tarred road sticking to your feet. All at once, you're at a woman's door, proposing marriage, signing divorce papers, giving a fifth of Scotch to the new husband, who's on his way out the door with a cocktail waitress. The past keeps piling up. There isn't enough room for it all.

Anne wants the world to work. Her second choice is to understand why it almost never does. She wants to know why she got married, why she got divorced. Why my reaction to the world is always so much milder than hers.

"Things don't seem to bother you," she says. "I wonder if that's true or if you're just not saying."

"I don't know," I say.

"You know," she says. "You're too nice to people. Underneath, you might be Mr. Ego. You're probably completely indifferent to everybody around you."

"Could be true," I say, "except who cares what you think?"

We laugh, but then she says, "That's what I mean. You turn it into a joke. I want to know." She's chewing the corner of her mouth, something she does when she's thinking or worried.

"People just don't bother me," I say.

"Of course they do," she says, "and you owe it to them to get pissed off."

We're having our afternoon drink at a bar called Ned's Gator or something. When the bartender comes to our table, he leans on his elbows and stares at Anne with big watery eyes, smiling. When he goes away, she says, "What's his problem? I don't like this. Now everything's ruined."

I say, "Maybe he's high."

"Ruined."

"Or maybe he's in love."

She slaps the table and laughs her big throaty laugh. People turn and stare. "What's the matter? They never heard somebody laugh before?"

Anne's metaphor for a world that works is the Good Bar. A place where they know you well enough to bring your drink before you ask, but not so well that they kid you about how often you're there. Not too crowded. Not too empty. The light's just right and the music is old. A place where you can meet somebody who won't turn out to be an ax murderer. This is not too much to expect from the world.

When I first met her, I thought she was moody and overcritical. Nothing pleased her. Later I understood her better. She wants a kind of purity not found in nature.

"My ideal," she says, "is to live in one room with nothing but a rug, a chair, and a lamp."

Her real problem is that she can see the dark side of so

much that seems good. This is why she suspects the motives for my indiscriminate kindness. She writes about what she calls "deadly virtues" — integrity, honesty, loyalty. Maybe even kindness. She wonders if I tolerate people I don't like as a subtle way of ignoring them. I wonder, too.

I see her standing in the doorway between two rooms — one has a rug, a chair, and a lamp; the other is full of people. Sometimes the empty room is lonely. Sometimes the people stare when she laughs. To choose one room means losing whatever is good about the other. As philosophy, the dilemma is unattractive, an ugly duckling. It lacks irony. It's not as intricate as the Escher prints on her walls, not as elegant as the Wittgenstein she likes to quote, not as raw as the Hank Williams she punches up on the jukebox. But it's true.

Her territory is the threshold between choices. If she were lost in the woods and saw her own tent through the trees, what would she think? Would she be relieved that she had found her way home? Or disappointed that her courage had not carried her away? Probably both.

At dinner, Tbor keeps making cryptic references to the game. "Explain it or shut up," she says, and laughs.

"It's simple," he says, his voice solemn. "Characters can have different ethical alignments. Neutral evil, lawful evil, chaotic evil. Neutral, lawful, and chaotic good. Even neutral, lawful, and chaotic neutral." His look becomes sly. "Most of the time, I'm lawful good. But not always." I'm wondering if I'm chaotic neutral or just neutral neutral.

Somehow Aldebaran shook off his paralysis and lured

Tbor into a room with moving walls of flame. But Tbor, who's now Ossian the Ungood, trapped Aldebaran with an enchanted gaze, giving him only two choices: save himself by becoming Ossian's slave, or let Ossian's gaze turn him to stone. Aldebaran chose stone. I can tell from his voice that Tbor is disappointed and a little amazed at his friend's choice. We always are, I suppose.

The job I interviewed for is a good one but would keep me busy all the time. When I'm not lost in the woods with my survival class, I'd be prowling the dorm, sniffing for marijuana. If I don't get the job, I don't know what I'll do. If I do get it, the same. Either choice is the wrong one. Or the right one. I'm neutral neutral about it.

What's my ethical alignment regarding Anne? Chaotic neutral or just neutral neutral? And which is better? If you don't react when the bartender stares at the woman you're with, does it mean you're secure or indifferent? In the end, ethical alignment, like luck, probably doesn't come in flavors.

Sunday morning is lazy. A week of false spring has ended, bringing back the cold and snow. We get a fire going in the fireplace and sit on the floor in front of it to read. I drink cider and Anne smokes. We don't say much, but we're both thinking the same thing — we didn't find it. No epiphany, no dark cloud crackling with light; the scales have not fallen from our eyes. In the morning, when we wake up, we'll be the same people. How sad to be no wiser than we are. To walk into the wilderness of the new day and lose our way again.

Later she drives me to the bus station, giving me a

thumbs-up when I wave to her from the window. And then the bus pulls out and she's gone in a blur of gray-green hills and trees. I'm sorry to leave this shabby landscape behind — the fields lying like abandoned rugs, the sudden rivers and small streams edged with ice. I'm sorry to feel our weekend slipping away, becoming a memory that someday will seem strange and not at all like us. What will we think when we look back? Will we shake our heads at how we were so close to home and still so lost? We love each other. What question does that answer? Which fate do we fear most? Save or turn to stone? In the seat ahead of me sits a blind woman. Over and over, she sweeps her hand across the window, as though she can read the landscape through the cold glass.

The Hazards of Poetry

I HAVE NOT ALWAYS BEEN THE HARDWARE KING of the Shenandoah Valley. There was a time when I thought my life would turn out quite differently. It began one day when my father locked up his hardware store for the last time, went home, and quietly died. A life full of hardware will do that to a man. Behind me were two failed careers, a failed marriage, even a failed childhood. Only poetry had stayed true to me. Before me lay the life of a literary artist. I dropped my father into a hasty grave, sold the store, and set out for Europe, for Venice. What better place for my new life than Venice, the city of my literary father, Lord Byron, who spent his "year of revelry" there in 1817?

From the start, things did not go well. The crossing was a nightmare. I complained without success to the captain of the Liberian freighter (a touch of economy, a touch of romance) about the ship's violent pitching and the steady diet of boiled cabbage and potatoes. He replied, "To me you are so much freight, and freight does not complain."

Venice, too, was not what I had imagined. Instead of palazzos with grand colonnades, polished travertine, and magnificent frescoes, I saw a dilapidated city dissolving into fetid canals. Everything was full of dampness and dreariness, a wedding reception where the bride and groom had never arrived. Perhaps I should have left for home then and there. Perhaps I was right to stay. The human heart is hard to understand.

Byron had taken up residence in "remarkably good apartments" just off the Piazza San Marco, not to mention his villa at La Mira. The best I could manage was a pair of drafty rooms in a distant backwater of the city. My heart sank as I inspected my shabby quarters. I was bitterly reminded of my ocean voyage by the sluggish lapping of the canal beneath my window.

"You will be fine," the concierge said, "until the winter tide comes." She felt pity for the sallow young man in his tight green velvet suit and pale yellow cravat.

After spending the first two days recuperating from my voyage, I summoned the will to venture forth. When I stepped out onto the crumbling steps of my *pensione* in midmorning of that third day, two gondoliers nearly knocked me into the canal, butting their water taxis against the steps. My Italian was poor. Like Byron, I preferred French. I climbed aboard the nearest boat. The gondolier had massive arms and tobacco stains running down the front of his jaunty red-and-white-striped jersey. The other boatman hissed an obscenity and swung his shiny hearse into the current. I was ferried more or less against my will to the

Piazza San Marco, because, the boatman explained as he spat tobacco juice into the canal, "that is where all good tourists go."

I made the best of it, even though the piazza was not Byron's favorite place. For a while, I even walked with a slight limp, imagining myself the maimed poet forced to stroll against his will among the crowds of tourists. A cramp settled into my leg, so I gave it up. I bought a fresh loaf of bread and nibbled serenely as I admired *la famosa quadriglia* of the basilica.

Suddenly, a flock of pigeons swept down upon me. I couldn't move. People turned to watch. Cameras clicked. It was as if I were one of the sights they had come to see. I swung the loaf wildly in self-defense. Hopeless. Flapping wings cut the air in front of me. High throaty gurgles nearly drove me mad. In desperation, I flung the bread at the flock and ran for the sanctuary of the doge's palace.

Touring had had enough of me that day, and so, watchful for another winged assault, flinching at every flying shadow, I made my way to the edge of the canal. I hailed each passing boat. Their drivers waved back placidly and floated on. Then, as if by magic, balanced on the bobbing deck of his boat, arms folded over his broad chest, his chew of tobacco puffing his sweaty cheek to the size of a healthy lemon, stood the boatman I had hired that morning. "Good tourist," he cooed as I fearfully climbed aboard.

That night did not pass well for me. I was kept awake by the steady thrum and throb of motor launches in the canal outside my window. Each time a boat went by, the few moored to the wall below my window scudded and bumped against the building. My bed felt like a heap of damp laundry. A deep-green carpet of mold clung to the corners of the ceiling, and from my window I could not see the moon.

The days passed and my melancholy grew. Sometimes, when the nights were long, I would read my Byron, especially the letters from Venice. "I am always in copulation," he wrote to his sister. Are there more rapturous syllables in any language? Poetry and passion were inextricably linked in my young mind. I decided there was but one balm for my ailing heart.

And so, while having coffee at an open-air café on the piazza one afternoon, I fell in love. The waitress serving my table was small, olive-skinned, and ignored me completely. No matter how often I shook my napkin at her, I could not catch her eye. Finally I stood, cleared my throat, and took a step toward her. She turned. For one heady moment I could not speak, intoxicated as I was by her dark eyes, her Mediterranean indifference, and her mysterious scent, which I would later describe in a poem called "Beguiled by Calvin Klein's Infinity." At last I muttered, "Have a nice day," and rushed madly into the crowd, crippled with joy.

My soul shot heavenward. I imagined the dark-eyed stranger as mine. She would turn out to be a contessa wrongfully done out of her fortune in some family intrigue. I, an American poet on holiday, would publish an epic in the newspapers that would praise her nobility and expose the wrongdoer — an uncle, I imagined, who had altered her father's will. How else could she repay me but with love everlasting?

Later, in the midst of another such reverie, I found her at a souvenir vendor's cart strung with plastic gondolas. She was a proud, frail beauty in cashmere and denim. She was having trouble choosing a color.

I gazed up at the *quadriglia* and said, "It seems to me, at times like these, when the light shines on them just so, that the golden horses are ready to take flight." I was thrilled with my sudden erudition.

"They're fakes," the waitress said in a decidedly un-Mediterranean accent. "The real ones got eaten up by the smog." A New Jersey accent.

An undistinguished meeting, you say? But it was enough. I had gone from exhilaration to ecstasy. I was in love. Venice was mine. I thought of Byron discovering his dark-eyed beauty in the streets of Venice. "I have found you, my Marianna Segati," I murmured, my eyes filling with joy and with little tears.

"The name is Cindy," she said pulling her hand away from my lips, "and I was never lost."

It turned out that she was a student at a croupier school, a blackjack major. I insisted that she allow me to act as her guide to Venice. I took her for a stroll along the loggia of the doge's palace. I said, "Next we will go to Tintoretto's *Last Supper.*"

She said, "I missed lunch. I could do with a bite." To her look of disappointment and her moan of hunger as we stood before the painting, I smiled paternally and said, "A feast for the eyes, like your sweet self, my dear."

Her eyes widened with fear and anger. I stared into them

and whispered, "Cynthia, oh Cynthia, my constant moon." She turned from me. She fled, casting the word "wacko" upon the late-afternoon breeze.

"Forgive me!" I cried, but it was too late.

In the days that followed, I spent every afternoon with her, in a fashion. I would sit in her section of the café, simply for the privilege of being near her. I wrote poems of unsurpassed beauty and recited them in my best basso profundo as she passed with orders for other tables.

All to no avail.

After a few days, I grew desperate for her attention. I ordered cup after cup of espresso. *"Più !"* I cried. "More!" I had to drink a prodigious amount of the potent concoction, but my love was by my side — scowling, but by my side — the lip of the espresso pot poised over my cup.

It was then that the brute who managed the café discharged her.

He said, "You ignore the other customers to linger on your lover." (Would that it were so!) "With us your job is finished!"

The reply she uttered defies description.

In the ensuing confusion, somehow the espresso pot was emptied into my lap. She stamped off. I tried to follow, but the manager stopped me with a bill for twenty thousand lire.

"Who can put a price on love?" I said, emptying my wallet onto the table.

When I caught up with my outraged beloved, she met me with a torrent of abuse. I was, she said, scum.

"A man in love does many things," I explained.

"Try suicide," she said.

We passed our afternoon this way, with a steady exchange of sentiments. In the end I persuaded her to share my quarters until she could find another job. She had only two conditions: that she be allowed to bring her pet, Meryl, and that there be "no funny business." Dear reader, my love was no laughing matter.

And so it was that Cynthia moved in with me, bringing all her worldly possessions: a collection of Raggedy Ann dolls and Meryl, a morose chimpanzee with matted hair. The strength of my devotion would not allow me to acknowledge the discomfort I felt as I stood beside the loathsome beast. I forced myself to smile instead.

Cynthia, my constant moon, moved in on a Friday. She and I stayed indoors all weekend. Later we learned that we were the talk of the canal. Everyone told stories about the strange whoops and shrieks that issued from my rooms. People shook their heads and smiled at the mad passion of the young. Actually, the sounds were coming from the chimpanzee, who found the move a difficult affair. She charged us every time we tried to go out, so we stayed huddled together under the blanket, clinging to each other for safety.

There, starving and fearful in our woolen cocoon, I witnessed the dawning of her affection.

She said, "You're not half bad when you're out of those funny clothes and down off your high horse."

Dear reader, you may surmise what followed those treasured words, but modesty compels me to draw the curtain here.

Eventually we trapped Meryl in the closet, and as the weeks unfolded, Venice became "the pleasant place of all festivity" that Byron had promised me. We doted on each other, and when we tired of that, we doted on Venice. My passion was for Cynthia, poetry, and art, while hers was for restaurants, boutiques, chocolate, movies, records, dancing, her ape, and me.

I surprised her one afternoon with a doll shelf I had made from a fruit crate. "I like presents," she said, "but what about something in the line of jewelry?" Another time, I bought a red leather leash for the acrid-smelling Meryl, who promptly chewed it to pieces. Despite these setbacks, O reader, my love grew.

When the Festival of the Redeemer came, we celebrated by spending the night in a gondola on the lagoon. We spoke in whispers on the dark water until dawn. I told her I would be glad to die if I could write just one immortal poem. She looked at me, her eyes damp with desire, and said, "I want to be a star."

But as quickly as it had risen, my moon set. One moment we were shopping happily at an open-air market. The next, my beloved was making plans to fly back to the States. She had received a telegram. Her family, it turned out, had been invited to discuss her brother's sex-change operation on a television talk show. "This is only the beginning," she said breathlessly. "It's my chance to break into the big time! I'll probably get my own series pretty soon."

Foolish me. I thought *I* was her "big time." A quickly

packed suitcase, a hasty farewell, and she was gone, leaving me with Meryl.

My depression was unfathomable. Winter was coming. Venice spent much of the time under a pale fog, inventing endless shades of gray. In my grief I rarely stirred from my rooms, eating only one meal a day, a loaf and a bottle of wine, which I shared with the inconsolable chimpanzee. The beast huddled among the Raggedy Ann dolls, whimpering, petting each doll until strands of red yarn littered the floor. Byron, I remembered, said that falling in love was the next-best or -worst thing to falling in the canal.

Where were the scandals and the horrors and the *soirées à la mode*? The aging and lascivious dowagers and the young contessas? The hot brandy punch, wild duck, and stewed venison? The ladies of rank and mystery who had, perhaps, stilettoed a lover or two? On what blessed patch of ground was my moon shining?

The regatta came and went, but I had lost my taste for celebration. I remembered Byron's words: "I stood in Venice, on the Bridge of Sighs, a palace and a prison on each hand. . . ."

Each evening, when I first came to Venice, the sun would drop its rose over the city. But now the late afternoons had turned colder, and night came on like a torch being plunged into the murky Adriatic. With winter, the canals began to rise. I knew this by the increasing dampness of my rooms. Puddles of water had begun to collect in the corners. Even when I ventured outside, a melancholy stroll across the piazza was impossible, now that it lay ankle deep in water and crisscrossed by a network of catwalks.

Venice, too, was washing her hands of me.

It was to the darkest, most forsaken parts of the city that Meryl and I would take our walks. Sometimes, in those closing days of my season of sorrow, we'd spend half the night on the wharf, staring at the huge shadows of the tankers in the lagoon, while Meryl searched herself for lice, thoughtfully sniffing and chewing each one. We'd let the night gather us into itself, silence all about except for the lapping of the water and the faint gurgling of the chimpanzee's stomach. I'd think about Byron, of a century when things happened as they were supposed to.

One morning the concierge burst into my room as I slept.

"Cynthia!" I cried out in my confusion.

"Run or be drowned!" the old woman screamed, clapping her hands to her cheeks and racing off. The canal was streaming through the open window and fanning gracefully across the room. Meryl leaped onto my narrow bed, an armload of soggy dolls clutched to her hirsute bosom. Just then I heard the roar of a motor launch, and the canal gushed into the room, sweeping the furniture against the walls. Fish flung themselves onto the floor. Stranded on the bed as the water rose around us, we two pathetic primates shivered with fear.

It was then that I thought of hardware.

Perhaps my father was right, I thought. Perhaps I should move back to the States, to a small town in the country, with several vowels in its name. I could open a large store on a quiet street, a wonder of whitewash and plate glass.

The water rose, my night table floated away, the prow of a gondola poked through the open window.

After all, I thought, as Meryl slipped her thin leathery hand into mine, isn't there finally something comforting about nails carefully separated into bins? About wrenches ranked in order of size? Something terribly beautiful about drop-forged steel?

All I Ever Wanted

I WAS DRIVING TRUCK FOR FRIEDMAN TRANSFER when Rachel sold her baby. It's funny what you remember. The things that stay and the things that fade. What I remember most is our trailer. The way the wind whanged it around. The way the rain poured in, turning the paneling into wet cardboard, the rug into oatmeal. That place was a joke. It was a bad time. A bad time all around.

The only freight Friedman carried was a daily newspaper that came out at two-thirty or so. The exact time depended on how many blow-ins there were that day. Store ads, sheets of coupons, that kind of stuff. We'd get to work at twelve, in case of an early press run, and play Tri-Ominos until we got the call. It passed the time and kept us out of fights. Then we'd load up and locate our bundle boys, a bunch of dropouts who spent every free minute behind the building smoking dope.

Mine was named Sammy. I remember he was saving up for a Fender Stratocaster. Sometimes, on the road, I'd look back into the box and see him playing air guitar like he was

57

on MTV. He was so into it he always tossed off the bundles at the wrong corners. Those poor carriers never knew where they'd find their papers.

We were paid for four hours' work, even though we only worked two, and the four-hour pay was more than most got for eight. It was a lazy man's job, a good job.

Things started to go bad when the pressmen at the newspaper went out on strike. They were losing their jobs to automation, so who could blame them? But we drivers decided not to sympathy strike, because the pressmen didn't support us last time we went out. Nobody remembered that, though, so the whole town turned against us. Guys waited for us at the drop-off points. Sammy'd pitch out a bundle of papers, they'd pitch it right back into the truck. They'd throw rocks. They'd cuss us out. Most of them were Polish. When somebody swears at you in a language you don't understand, it does things to your head.

They were a strange bunch, those Polish. Most of them were retired miners. Esther is a coal town at the foot of the Poconos. About twenty years ago, the river broke through the roof of a tunnel here. At the mouth of the cave-in there was a whirlpool wide as a city block. So big the coal company ran a line of boxcars into it to stop it up, but they were sucked underground without a trace. The river kept pouring in until every shaft and tunnel under the valley was flooded.

That killed coal in Esther, but the Polish stayed on. No real jobs. No money. The ground cracking open under your house and no insurance to cover it. They stayed anyway. Everything that ever meant anything to them was underground, flooded, out of reach, but they stayed on. I think they must've gone crazy. They lived and died by the union, and in the end, not even that could save them. Maybe they saw the strike as a way to get something back. Still, I can't feature it.

I was never much of a drinker, but every week the strike violence was getting worse, so I started stopping by this southside bar after work, just to settle my nerves.

That's where I met Rachel, at Donahue's Hourglass. She was a licensed practical nurse. Thin blond hair and a bony face. Bony but attractive. After a while I was seeing her there every afternoon. We'd talk. We'd drink. We'd eat a little bar food. We were together so much the regulars treated us like a couple, which I guess was OK with me.

Rachel and I got to know each other through the things we hated. "Whining and dining," we called it. As soon as we sat down we'd start moaning about our day. She liked the old people she took care of in the nursing home, but some of them were zombies. They were the ones I wanted to hear about. The one that called her "Mama." The one that spent the night in the john because he couldn't find the door.

I'd tell her the latest strike stuff. How somebody sprayed "Scabs" on the door of the truck barn and punctured all the tires. The newspaper set up round-the-clock security. Big guys with dogs and guns and ax handles. I don't know who scared me more.

One night, two weeks after we met, after the last last call, Rachel put down her drink and said, "Well? What about it?" We were both of us at that point where you think all the hard questions can be settled only in the dark, with your clothes off. "Yeah," I said hoarsely. "I'd like that. I'd like that a lot."

She was too drunk to drive, so we left her Volkswagen in the parking lot. When we pulled away in my screechy Impala, I said, "I think my ball joints are shot."

She looked at me funny and said, "We'll see. We'll see." I liked her for that.

She told me she lived in the country. Some joke. She lived in a trailer park on the edge of town. In an empty cornfield across the highway was some kind of hobo village — pickups with homemade plywood campers built on the back, beat-up motor homes.

"Gypsies," she said when she saw me staring. "Sometimes I go over, have a cup of coffee, shoot the shit. They're all right. The queen's in the hospital here. They're waiting for her to die."

I saw a school bus with bubble windows. On top was a sundeck with a picket fence. Inside, there were flickering lights and the shadows of people dancing. Somehow it didn't seem right.

The first thing I saw in Rachel's trailer was a crib in the corner of the living room, a lump under the blanket. She turned back the cover a little and I could see this sleeping baby — the chubby cheeks, the high round forehead, the pouty lips.

I said, "Is it yours?"

"No," she whispered, her eyes going wide. "I got her with box tops. What do you *think*?" She said her name was Trish.

We stood there for a few seconds watching her sleep, her little hands curled up like flowers.

Rachel led me to the sofa. At first we sat there in silence. Then she got up and poured us a couple of bourbons. Neither one of us knew how to talk without a drink in our hands.

She said, "Technically, I guess I'm still a married woman. A little after Trish was born, my old man came home all pumped about the army. Said he could make more working for Uncle Sam than he could installing car stereos." She shook her head and sipped her drink. There were dark smudges under her eyes. It was late. Her voice was low because of the baby.

"For a week I did nothing but get him ready to go. I cleaned and ironed all his clothes, bought him new underwear, new socks. And all the while he's telling me about his plans — how he's going to make sergeant, how we're going to raise Trish in a big house on the base, and this, this, this. Before he got on the bus he said, 'What if I can't cut it at boot camp?' It was like he was all of a sudden my kid. I said, 'You're tough, Lenny, and you're smart. You'll do fine.' When I kissed him goodbye, the tears came shooting out of my eyes."

Now I saw that all our stories about nursing home zombies and maniac strikers were nothing but practice for the stories that really mattered. I sat there holding tight to that jelly glass of bourbon, listening as hard as I could.

She said, "When I didn't hear from him for a month, I called Fort Bragg, where he went for basic, but they said they never heard of him. The recruiting office in town told me he never even enlisted." She shook her head. She sat there looking into her glass like something dead was floating around in there. She said, "Can you believe it?" She looked up at me. "Have you ever in all your life heard anything so stupid?" I couldn't tell if she meant what Lenny did or how she believed him.

I said, "My dad was in the service." I didn't know what else to say. I touched her arm with my thumb, the soft skin inside her elbow. "You're better off without the guy. The service turned my dad into a nutcase. He'd come home on leave and bat me around just for the hell of it." I showed her the little finger of my left hand. He broke it so many times when I was a kid, it's shorter than the other one and hooked away from the hand a little. I can't even bend it. She leaned over and kissed the finger, then my open palm. Light, quick kisses, but they gave me the chills. I kissed her hair. It smelled of shampoo and cigarettes. Then our mouths were all over each other and we stopped talking.

I pretty much moved in that night. Partly because I felt sorry for her. Partly because I was living in a moldy basement efficiency with one plate, one cup, one spoon. But mainly because she just made me feel good. It was like we saw the world with the same eyes.

And I liked Trish. She wasn't even a year old, too little to know what to make of me. When Rachel went out to the store, I danced around the room with her up against my shoulder. We danced to Elvis, Buddy Holly. The classics.

Every once in a while she'd rear back her wobbly head and look at me like I was a talking dog. She made me laugh out loud. She was a good baby.

I don't know why I didn't carry on like that when Rachel was around. I think it was the way she looked at the baby. She loved her and all, but it was like she couldn't look at her without thinking of Lenny, what he did to her.

Things were fine for a couple months. During the days, while we were at work or at The Hourglass, one of the Gypsy women came and sat with Trish, an old woman named Andrea, who had a big cracked mouth and gray hair that hung way down her back. Their queen was taking a long time to die, and a lot of the Gypsies were desperate for any kind of work they could find.

When winter came on, the strike turned ugly. One day I was creeping my truck up a narrow, winding street. Esther is nothing but hills. Not a level spot anywhere. On streets like that, fourth gear is a fantasy. You hardly even see third. No real clearance. Those streets were made for donkey carts, not twenty-four-foot panel trucks. It's first gear all the way, which is strange. On most trucks, you never touch first. But not in Esther. If you meet somebody head-on, one of you has to back up to the last intersection and let the other one pass. You have to take the turns in installments. That job gave me a round tailbone and an ulcer.

When I looked up to check for traffic, a guy was standing in the street ahead of me, an old man in green work pants, a big man with a face like a fist. Before I knew what was happening, he threw a rock at my windshield. Glass flew everywhere. My knuckles got all cut up. It happened so fast I didn't even have time to take my hands off the wheel.

"You *scob!*" the man yelled, waving his fist at me. "You go straight from stinking hell, you *scob!*"

A few weeks after that, Rachel lost her job. The state was phasing out the L.P.N., so the nursing home had to let her go. She tried to get another job, but it was the same story everywhere — R.N. or nothing. She stopped looking for work and stayed home with Trish. She started drinking more. A little eye-opener in the morning. A little something with lunch. And then some serious drinking in the evening. We had to sell her V-Dub, so she couldn't even meet me at The Hourglass anymore. But I don't think she even wanted to. The Gypsy woman, Andrea, hung around the trailer all the time now, getting drunk with her on jug wine.

The L.P.N. meant a lot to her. She got it after Lenny left, in a special job-training program. She only wanted to change her luck, do some good, make a little money. And for a while that's what happened. But then they took it away from her. They just ripped it right out of her hands. Who could blame her for drinking?

Across the highway, more Gypsies showed up every day. Broken-down cars and trucks were parked all over the corn-field. News was spreading about the queen. Some of the Gypsies were camped out in the hospital room and wouldn't let the regular doctors and nurses treat her. She didn't have much longer.

To make things worse, that winter was the hardest the valley'd seen in twenty years. One morning we woke up to two feet of snow outside and the furnace dead. Like waking up in a deep freeze. Rachel was lying there staring at the ceiling. I could see her breath. Her lips were a little gray. Almost like she was talking to herself, she said, "It's not supposed to be like this."

I went down the hall and kicked and swore at the furnace until I could get the pilot relit, but that was just the beginning. In the john I found two-inch plugs of ice poking out of the sink and bathtub drains. The whole plumbing system was rock solid with ice. Even the water in the toilet bowl had a skin of ice on it. I started outside with a hammer to bang on the pipes, but the door was frozen shut. I had to kick it open.

I crawled under the trailer — stray cats bawling and hissing at me from the dark corners — but no amount of banging on the pipes would free them up. Then I got a brainstorm. I saw an old bag of self-starting charcoal briquettes and lined them up under the pipe. The whole length of the trailer. I lit them, hoping there would be enough flame to free up the pipe but not enough to burn down the trailer. When I heard the rattle of the ice breaking up and the sound of the water flowing, I felt like a goddamn genius.

I went back inside the trailer to brag to Rachel. She was standing by the front door in her bathrobe, aiming the blow dryer at the hinges. They were iced up so bad the door wouldn't close. Her mouth was a hard line.

I told her how I worked on the pipe. I said, "What would you do without me?" I was kidding.

She stared back at me with a dead flat look in her eye, like maybe she knew the exact answer to that question. Like it was me who brought the blizzard and got her laid off and made Lenny leave. Like it was my fault for everything.

All I ever wanted was a paycheck and a little peace. But things keep coming at you. They turn you around.

Later that day I was driving my truck up Madison, a hill that won't quit. My eyes were on the side mirrors. I was taking it slow, watching my clearance. There was barely a whisper between me and the parked cars. The engine was aching, overheated. I stopped at the top of the hill and waited for Sammy to put down his air guitar and toss off three bundles of papers.

At first I didn't know what was going on. I heard a sound like a big wind. Then the little window behind the cab was full of bright orange light. I set the brake hard and ran to the back of the truck. Somebody had thrown a bottle bomb inside. Thick black smoke whirled out of the truck, and everywhere flames. Sammy was inside, his back to one wall, just staring at the fire, too scared to move. His eyebrows were singed off, and his hair was smoking. His face was bright red. He fought me when I tried to get him out. I had to slap him some.

When the firemen came and saw it was a Friedman truck, they just stood there and let it burn. Flaming scraps of paper tumbled across the icy ground. Black flakes of ash sailed over the housetops.

By now the paramedics had put Sammy on a stretcher. His eyes were big and scared. "Did my shirt get burned?" he said, trying to look down at his Guns N' Roses T-shirt. "It's my brother's. If it's wrecked, he'll kill me."

They put him in the ambulance and drove him away. The firemen stood around in black and yellow raincoats, smoking and joking, watching my truck burn down.

I yelled, "I never did one fucking thing to you people!"

They just stood there smiling. One of them flipped me off.

I walked all the way back to Friedman's. I didn't even explain what happened. Just got in my car and went straight to the state store, then parked behind the Super Saver on Northampton, trying to calm down, trying to think.

When my pint was gone, I drove back to the trailer. They were sitting at the kitchen table, a jug of red wine between them. The old woman was talking quietly. Her hands were lying open on top of the table. Rachel sat staring into them, shaking her head slightly, a grim look in her eye. When I walked in, they stopped talking and looked away, like I caught them planning a robbery.

All the taps in the trailer were trickling so the pipes wouldn't freeze again. The space heater was turned on its end and propped next to the hinges of the front door. Trish was in the crib, booming her heels against the mattress and crowing.

I said, "I'm quitting my job."

Rachel said, "So? It was a shit job anyway." Then she and Andrea looked at each other, their secret hanging in the air between them. I felt like a stranger.

"You got to be kidding," I said. "That was the dream job of my life."

She laughed. "Driving a truck?" She laughed again, louder. There was nothing funny about that laugh. It put a million miles between us. She was trying to tell me something, to tell herself something maybe, something that would wipe away all our talk about strikes and nursing home zombies, something that would take her back to who she was before hard luck got hold of her.

I said, "We need a drink."

Rachel gave me a cockeyed smile and raised her glass. "I'll drink to that."

"Not here," I said. "Out."

Andrea said, "I'll stay with *Treesh.*" It was the first time I ever really heard her talk out loud. Her voice was scratchy. Her accent was right out of a horror movie.

I drove us to The Hourglass. We didn't say anything the whole way, not until we sat down at the bar.

"Rachel," I said, "I've been thinking about things." I sipped my drink.

"What things?" She was already drunk. So was I, for that matter. She looked at me from a long way off, like she was getting ready to laugh again.

"You don't really want to know," I said.

She turned back to her wine. All right, suit yourself.

I said, "Texas." The echo of her laugh was still in my head. I wanted to hurt her for it. I was drunk and scared and stupid. "I'm thinking a lot about Texas."

She started chewing on the corner of her mouth. "Texas."

"Yeah. Things are going on down there. I'm just thinking, you know. But Texas, that's one of the things I'm thinking."

Rachel set down her glass. "What a*bout* Texas?"

"Jobs. You know. Opportunity. Money. I could work on one of the oil rigs in Galveston Bay."

"What do *you* know about oil?"

"Don't need to know a thing. It's grunt work. A guy-I-know's brother works on one. Six months he lives on the rig. He's on the drill crew, those big diamond-point drills. It's good money. He's got a real house. He's got a VCR."

"What am I supposed to do in Texas?" she said slowly.

"That's what I'm thinking," I said, nodding. "I'm thinking maybe I could go on ahead and get us set up first."

She didn't say anything. She just stared at me, her eyes ticking back and forth across my face.

"I know what you're thinking, Rachel, but it isn't like that. I mean, why should you come down now when you can come down later, after I get us a nice place?"

She took a sip of wine and looked at her face in the mirror behind the bar. I said, "I'll probably have to sleep in my car for a while."

She set the glass down gently, then slid it slowly across the bar, to the back edge, a little over, farther.

I said, "Is that what you want for Trish? Living in a car?"

She shot me a look, and I knew I had gone too far. She tipped the glass over the side. It broke against the edge of the sink. The bartender was about to say something, but the look in her eye cooled him.

She stood up slowly, holding onto the bar rail. She clapped her other hand on my shoulder and said, "You have yourself a good old time, cowboy."

"It's not what —"

"Oh, shut up," she said, and headed for the door.

I followed her out into the snowy parking lot.

I grabbed her by the shoulder and turned her to me. Her eyes were shiny and hard. "I'm not Lenny, Rachel." That's what I said, but I felt exactly like him. "I'm just trying to do the best thing." I thought it was the truth. I wanted to believe it. But she knew me too well. Me or the world.

She said, "Just go. Just leave me alone." She pulled away and ran to the car, her boots slipping on the ice.

I yelled, "I was almost killed today!" I held out my hands like a begging dog. I wanted her to see my cut-up knuckles and my forearms, red and stinging, the arm hairs burned all off. But my knuckles weren't bad, and my arms only looked sunburned. "Do you care? No! You don't care!"

She was almost at the car. She spun around. "Scab!"

"You *nev*er cared about me!"

"That's right, scab! You were nothing to me! You hear? Nothing!"

"Fuck you!"

"No, fuck *you!*"

She stomped over to the passenger side of the car, dug out her keys, got inside, and flung the door shut. I dug out my set of keys and got in behind the wheel. We just sat there staring out at the snow whipping across the icy parking lot. That's when I think we maybe could have saved it. For a second I think we both saw how funny we looked, how ridiculous. But then the second was gone. We slid right past it. Rachel moved over against the passenger door. She stared out the

70

side window as I drove us home through the frozen streets, smoky with snow.

I thought about things. Like how, after making love, she liked to whisper old songs to me. *My funny valentine, sweet comic valentine* ... And how I liked to take her for walks and tell her the names of stars and trees. I thought about these things and about all the other things that would never happen again.

It was late and cold when we got back. Rachel was out of the car before I even stopped. She ran into the trailer, then came outside with Andrea. At the end of our lane, they stepped over the guardrail and crossed the highway. They walked carefully through the frozen corn stubble. There were fewer cars in the Gypsy camp now. I guess the queen was finally dead and they were moving on. Two more left while I stood there. One of them was the bus with bubble windows. When it drove past, I could see small lighted chandeliers swinging from the ceiling and oil paintings hanging on the walls.

I went into the trailer and poured myself a drink. I checked on Trish. She was sleeping scrunched up in the corner of her crib. I whispered, "I guess we won't be dancing anymore, will we, little one?" She'd get over this, I figured. Hell, she wasn't even a real person yet. Right? I tried to remember where all my stuff was and what would be the quickest way to get it all together. Before I knew it, Rachel was back. She was yelling at me from outside.

"Andrea's right!" she yelled. She pronounced the name like it belonged to a movie star. "Ruin! Ruin follows in your wake." Her voice was shaky and full of crying.

I went outside, yelling, "You think I like this?" I flung my arm out at the trailer. "You think this is the way I want things to be?" A light came on next door.

She'd brought some Gypsies with her. Andrea stood next to her on our cement slab. Behind them, two men stood in the shadows. She ran inside the trailer, leaving me with the Gypsies. The men were standing right in the flower bed I had dug around the slab last fall. It was ice and frozen mud now, but all I could think of was how I sifted that dirt through a wire screen and mixed it with compost. How I set the roots so the eyes were just belowground. In the spring there'd be peonies where they were standing.

Trish's eyes were big and dark and sleepy. Rachel had her wrapped in an old afghan. She held her tight against her chest. Then she gave her to the old woman.

I made a move toward Rachel. "What are you doing? Don't do this."

One of the men slipped away as soon as Rachel came out. I tried to see the other guy's face, but the shadows were too deep. I said, "Get the fuck off my peonies."

He stepped forward, into the light from the open door. He was an old man in work clothes, with a sweaty handkerchief knotted around his neck. Crooked over his left forearm was an open shotgun. I could see the butts of two shells in the breech. He pulled off his old felt hat with the other hand, like he was about to apologize. He set the hat on top of the breech and took a packet of money out of it.

He turned to Rachel, his voice quiet. "We agreed to five thousand dollars?"

Rachel looked down at her empty hands. I could hardly hear her when she said, "Yeah."

The old man stepped closer to her. There was no pupil in his right eye. What was left was like buttermilk. He held the money out to her.

She took it and said, "What about . . . ?"

He pointed to the icy, rutted lane that ran past the end of the trailer. An engine started up. When the headlights came on, we could see the other Gypsy sitting in a sports car, a little MG. It was deep green. The top was down. Once it was running, he got out, leaving the door open.

I said, "Rachel . . . Rache, you don't know what you're doing. You don't want to be doing this."

Her eyes were all red and sloppy. When she went inside the trailer, the old woman started to walk away with Trish. She said words to her in a language I couldn't understand.

"Andrea," I said. It was the first time I ever said her name, the first time I ever even spoke to her. I said her name the way Rachel said it. "Andrea, don't —" I started to follow her, but the old man stepped out, jerking the shotgun shut.

I pointed at it and said, "What's that? What's that for?"

It was just the two of us now. He looked down like he was seeing the gun for the first time. The wind picked up, ghosting snow off the tops of the trailers. "This?" he said, turning the gun barrel a little toward me. "This is nothing. This is for nothing."

Rachel came out of the trailer with a packed suitcase and headed for the car. She threw the suitcase into the passenger seat. The door went *chunk* when she closed it. She gunned the engine a couple times.

"Rachel," I yelled. "Trish —"

"You did this," she yelled, stabbing at me with her finger. *"You."* That's when I went for her. I didn't care about the shotgun anymore. I knocked the guy out of my way and went for her. She tried to shove the stick into first. I was almost on her when the back wheels spun against the ice and then caught. The car fishtailed as she took off, slamming sideways into some garbage cans.

I ran hard. Dogs were barking. Lights were coming on in the other trailers. I kept running. I thought I could catch her. She'd have to slow down, the lane curved so much. But she just threw that car into every turn, snow and ice shooting up behind her. Never slowed for a second.

I kept running. My chest was tight. My teeth felt like they were shaking loose. She swung out of the trailer park and onto the highway. Then she opened it up, and I knew it was all over. She took third to the top and ran wide open into fourth. In a few seconds she was out of sight. I stood there beside the road with my hands on my knees, heaving. She really drove. I stood there for a long time, trying to catch my breath, as the howl of that engine faded into the dark.

Haven't You Ever Seen Cary Grant?

"*Y*OURS?" EDNA PELKNER ASKED ONE MORNING when he answered the door. She was holding a pair of monkey-fist gloves. They were so filthy she held them in two fingers. With her other hand, she shaded her eyes from the early-September sun. Mark had never stood so close to her before. Her hair was the color of boiled cabbage. She wore it pulled tight against her scalp. Her mouth was a hard edge. Her face had barely enough skin to cover the bone.

Mark and Linda Butler had lived in the neighborhood for six months or so, and until then they'd only nodded to their neighbors. When the old woman appeared at their door, Mark considered it a broken vow of silence.

She held the gloves out, as if he couldn't see them well enough. The palms of both were scraped into a rough stubble of leather and grease. The curve of the thumb and forefinger on each was thick with grease. They looked like two obscenely deformed figs.

"Because if they are, I found them."

"Oh."

"In the road. There . . ." She pointed into the street. Her house faced his and Linda's. At the bottom of her driveway sat her blue Volkswagen Super Beetle, its small hood sprung open. On the sidewalk next to it sprawled a dark spill of gasoline. The car looked defiled.

"I don't understand," Mark said carefully.

"What's to understand? They're either yours or they're not."

"They're not mine."

"Of course they're not," she said, as if she'd known all along he would say that.

"Really."

"Then it's settled, right?" She wrung the greasy gloves in her hands, forgetting how filthy they were.

"I guess so."

"Settled. Ha!" She turned and walked stiffly back to her house. At the door, she dropped the gloves beside an ancient milk box, turned to look at him once more, then went inside, pulling the door shut as if it were the hatch cover of a diving bell.

"What was that?" Linda said, looking up from breakfast and the morning paper.

"Edna Pelkner. Something about some disgusting gloves."

"What's so disgusting about Old Widder Edna?"

"Not her. Her gloves."

"She's got a thing for you," Linda said.

"She's a senile old witch with filthy gloves."

"Come on," Linda said. "Lighten up. Don't get the way you get."

"What way?"

"You know. Look, she just put her husband in the ground. Give her a little patience."

That afternoon, when Mark came home from the junior college where he taught, Edna Pelkner's Super Beetle was still parked at the bottom of her hilly front lawn. The smear of gasoline had become a shaggy crescent hooking across the sidewalk and into the street. As Mark watched, a taxi stopped and Edna climbed out, defiantly ignoring him.

Inside, Linda was washing three fist-shaped green peppers in the sink. On the counter were blueberries, a few stalks of rhubarb wrapped in cellophane, potatoes, and onions. "Great stuff at the farmers' market," she called over her shoulder as he came in.

"Edna Pelkner didn't even look at me just now."

"Oh, poor boy. Romance gone out of your life?"

"You know what I mean. It's not good when your neighbors dislike you."

"Since when do you care what other people think?"

Mark remembered how close he'd stood to Pelkner. Close enough to smell the talcum and lilac. Close enough to see the crusty rash on her cheekbones. He wanted to erase the memory by leaning his face into Linda's hair, by breathing in the light, warm scent of her hair.

The latch of the storm door snapped open, and someone knocked lightly at the front door.

On the flagstone step stood a Borough Hall policeman. His patrol car was parked near the VW. He was blond and clean-shaven. In fact, he looked barely old enough to be clean-shaven. The brown, honeycomb grip of his revolver was strapped into its black leather holster. He held his visored cap in his right hand, and in his left, less gingerly than Edna Pelkner had handled them, he held the grease-covered gloves. Over the policeman's shoulder, Mark could see the Pelkner curtains pinched back so she could see without being seen.

"There's been a theft reported in the neighborhood, Mr. Butler, and we're wondering if you know anything about these gloves."

"Not those gloves again. I told her they aren't mine."

"Do you know anything about that car?" he asked politely, nodding toward the VW.

"Yeah, Hitler invented it. What's all this about?"

After a moment, the policeman said, "Your neighbor Mrs. Pelkner has reported that someone has stolen the fuel pump from her car. You wouldn't know anything about that, now would you, Mr. Butler?"

Mark shook his head and said, "Look, I don't know a thing about it. What kind of thief wears gloves like that, anyway?"

Edna Pelkner stood in her open doorway now, in plain view, shading her eyes from the sun. Whenever Mark saw her, she seemed to be shading her eyes.

"Car can't get you anywhere without your fuel pump," the policeman went on.

"I wouldn't know."

"I figure maybe it wasn't really a theft at all. I think maybe somebody was just having some fun at a widow's expense, is all. Only now the joke's flat, and she wants her fuel pump back. You wouldn't know anything about that, would you?"

"What do I look like? I'm thirty-four years old. I'm an assistant professor up for tenure review. I don't even know what a fuel pump is."

The policeman glanced down at his shoes. "I want to deal with this on an adult level, Mr. Butler, and I'm sure you want to cooperate. Am I right? I've got to check into every possibility." He pouted slightly, making Mark sorry he'd raised his voice.

The policeman replaced his cap and shifted his gun belt. The leather strained and creaked. He looked across the street at the car. "Life is tough enough for our seniors, you know? If you hear anything, you'll call?"

"The nerve of her," Mark said that night, standing behind the blinds of the bedroom window and staring out at Edna Pelkner's moonlit house. "I can't get over it. And the worst is how polite that baby-faced creep was."

"Come to bed," Linda said sleepily. "Haven't you ever seen Cary Grant in *To Catch a Thief*? Thieves are glamorous. It's a compliment."

"She's there right now, peering out from behind the curtain."

"They wear black. They move over the rooftops like a quiet breeze. It is reported by some observers that on occasion they even sleep."

"The gall of that woman!"

"You used to be so much fun, Mark," she said, her voice full of sleep.

Hearing his name turned him from the window. His wife seemed so far away. And for a moment Mark wished things were the way they used to be when they were first married. They'd wake up slowly and find their arms and legs flung carelessly over each other. They'd lie there in the half-light, smiling at each other and breathing the same sweet darkness. But that was centuries ago. He sat by the window for a long time, coming to bed only when he knew from her breathing that she was in a deep sleep.

At breakfast Linda read the "Good Morning" section of the newspaper, where readers wrote in to praise and condemn their neighbors.

" 'I think it stinks,' " she read, " 'the way a certain so-called neighbor of mine who shall remain nameless — in his blue late-model Volvo with the torn leather seat covers — has stolen my fuel pump. He will rue the day — in his Jamestown Blue split-level with two maple trees in the front yard — that he ever tangled with me.' It's signed 'E.P.' They even print her address."

Mark jumped up from the breakfast table, knocking his chair backward. "That's it. This is too much."

"Sweetheart," Linda said, "I think I should buy dark glasses and take back my maiden name."

"Where do you get off thinking this is all so funny?"

"Because you're taking it entirely too seriously," she said. "You take everything too seriously these days."

"She's the one. Not me."

"Have you thought of going over and talking to her? Just talking to her?"

There was a knock at the door. He quickly crossed the living room to answer it, expecting either Edna Pelkner or a SWAT team. On the front step stood a red-faced, emaciated teenaged boy. He wore tight black jeans and a white T-shirt with the sleeves rolled back. The Walkman clipped to his shaved head hissed and sputtered. He dipped and bobbed and swung his hips to the music.

"Pour vous," he said, thrusting a folded sheet of paper toward Mark's chest. "Mrs. P. said it was OK, said you'd probably want to settle up."

"She what?" Mark opened the invoice and read: "Parts (fuel pump) and labor (Gary) — $74.00."

Gary said, "I'm sort of in business for myself, so I hope you don't mind cash."

"What?"

"Don't worry. I can give you a receipt." He pulled a worn pad of receipts from his back pocket.

"Who the hell does she think she is?"

Gary slipped his earphones down around his neck, where they hung like an amulet. "Well, somebody'd better pay me," he said through a strained smile.

Mark said, "I didn't steal her goddamn fuel pump." He flipped the invoice at Gary and slammed the door.

"Who the hell does she think she is?" Mark yelled toward the kitchen.

"Well, you don't have to be so mean about it," Linda said. "Anyway, I think she's got guts."

"But I didn't take her goddamn fuel pump."

"Sure?"

"Come on."

"Christmas is just a scant four months away. Maybe you wanted to surprise me with a little something in rhinestones and 10-W-40?"

Mark said, "Do you know your problem? Do you know your problem?" But instead of telling her, he gave out a short strangled gasp, grabbed his briefcase, and lunged for the front door.

Outside, he climbed into their Volvo, ashamed of the torn seat covers for the first time, and drove three blocks before noticing the folded pink invoice tucked carefully under the wiper blade on the passenger side.

When he came home that evening, the gloves were lying on his front step. Wearing a flowered dress and a choker of pearls, Edna Pelkner, a suburban Cerberus, stood in front of her car. Mark twitched the gloves aside with a stick and returned the Pelkner glower. On the sidewalk, a huddle of children stared fearfully at the neighborhood thief.

That night Mark stood at the bedroom window, murmuring to himself, "If I were a thief, my gloves would have some style. Buffed calfskin dyed a deep, lustrous black and studded with rubies."

Linda groaned into her pillow.

The Pelkner VW sat squat and blue at the top of the driveway in the crisp glare of a newly installed security light. The hood was open, a curled lip of contempt, the car poised for theft.

Mark could see the grease-covered engine cavity, thought he could see the new fuel pump, shinier than the rest, like an eye cast coldly at him. "Immaculate gloves with a silver clasp somewhere."

The next day, "Good Morning" carried several letters of sympathy for Pelkner. Two were from neighbors, who said they knew from the first that Mark was no good. Another had deduced from the description of the Volvo that Mark was her son's mass media teacher. She told how Mark had once borrowed an expensive pen from her son to sign something and had forgotten to return it. "Who forgets a thing like that?" she asked. "A crook, that's who."

Mark went through the day in alternating fits of rage and shame. He had the strong impression that his third-period class was laughing behind his back. He felt the same about his department colleagues at lunch. And the work-study part-timer who did his copying.

Late that afternoon his chair called him in to ask if his office phone was working. When Mark told her it was, she asked why his personal calls had been coming to her. A woman, she said, had been calling all day to ask about a fuel pump she said Mark was selling. At first he tried to explain. But when he realized the explanation would only complicate things, he just apologized and promised to keep his private business private.

Pelkner was ruining his life.

That evening Mark came home with a plan. When Linda met him at the door, he was carrying a large cardboard box.

"You got groceries?" Linda asked.

When Mark lifted the flaps and showed her the contents, she just looked at him for a few seconds and then left the room.

Inside were seventy pounds of tools and a half-dozen Volkswagen repair manuals. *Your VW and You, Getting to Know Your VW, Treat Your VW Right* — the book titles suggested that a personal relationship was possible with a Volkswagen. Among the tools were screwdrivers (flat blade, Phillips, and ratcheting), long-nosed pliers, slip-joint pliers, a set of box-end wrenches, a twelve-piece socket wrench set, a combination wrench set with a flex-head ratcheting drive handle and extensions, and a rubber mallet in case some stealthy whacking was necessary.

If Linda had offered him dinner, he would have refused it. She didn't offer. He spread the tools out on the living room rug and buried himself in *The Care and Feeding of Your VW.* Linda avoided him until about six-thirty when she came in putting on her jacket.

"Where are you going?" he asked.

"Out. A movie. It doesn't matter."

"What do you mean, it doesn't matter?"

"I mean I think you stink."

"What?"

"That poor woman —"

"Poor woman?"

"— was over here today, crying her eyes out. Ever since her husband died, the neighborhood kids have been robbing her apple tree, tipping over her garbage cans, breaking into her basement and stealing things." She zipped up her jacket. The zipper's sharp snigger cut the air.

"So?" Mark said. He didn't like the way things were going. Not one bit.

"They broke one of the boughs of her apple tree. She and her husband planted that tree together when they were newlyweds. Her husband loved that tree. Then she saw you steal her fuel pump. It was the last straw. It was late and hard to see, but she's pretty sure it was you."

"Is that why she's driving me crazy? Because some kid who looks like me boosted her fuel pump? It's that Vitali kid with the thyroid problem. Tell her that. Tell her to leave me alone."

"I told her. I said you're a decent man and kind, not a thief."

"Yeah."

"Only . . ."

"Only what?"

"Only, the way you've been acting lately, well, I don't know, Mark. She said whoever took it walked kind of funny. A little stiff. Hardly bending his knees. The way you walk."

Mark's eyes widened. "I don't walk funny. And anyway,

she called the chair today. Do you know how that makes me look? That's just the kind of thing that can blow tenure for me."

"I lied. I told her you were as torn up about it as she was. I told her it was probably someone from another neighborhood. But now ..." She nodded toward the pile of tools.

"I'm going to teach her a lesson," Mark said.

"Like last time?"

"What last time?"

"I'm going out."

"You're on her side."

"There aren't any sides here, Mark. I'm going out."

"When are you coming back?"

"Don't hold your breath."

"This is ridiculous. You're being ridiculous. You would side with that screwball instead of your own husband?"

"Those are books on car repair?" She pointed at the stack of manuals.

"Yeah."

"And those are tools?" The carpet glittered with chrome and drop-forged steel.

"Well, yeah."

"I don't know you anymore."

"This is nuts."

"And you love it." Her voice was trembling.

"Look, Linda," Mark said desperately. "If you go now, don't count on me being here when you get back."

"Mark, you haven't been here for a long time."

"Yeah, yeah, I know. I'm not the man you married. Well, nobody's the man you married."

Linda held her cupped hands together, as though she were waiting for Mark to set some delicate object in them. She was shaking.

She said, "Mark, what is happening to you?" But she didn't stay for an answer.

He wished she'd slammed the door when she went out, but she'd closed it quietly, as if she were a nurse leaving the room of a critically ill patient. He knew she wouldn't leave him. Something had just set her off. Some woman thing between her and the widow. She'd be back, all right. He returned to his manuals.

The fuel pump, he read, was a diaphragm pump that fed fuel to the carburetor. He read about the eccentric on the distributor drive shaft, which ran the thing. He read about the float bowl, the suction and delivery valves, the rocker mechanism, and the diaphragm pull rod. There was no way she would really leave him. And there was nothing wrong with the way he walked. He read about vacuums and flanges, about the diaphragm spring and the pump suction stroke. The fuel pump, he learned, was a precision instrument whose operation was fitted to the fraction of a millimeter. He studied photos and diagrams that made it look like a fishing reel from one angle, a space capsule from another. He learned to admire the simple elegance of the diaphragm and the way pressure built in the fuel line and pump chamber, the way the pump relentlessly fed fuel to the engine. He studied everything he could about the VW fuel pump. Everything except how to troubleshoot it, how to reassemble it, how to install it. He knew he would never need to know these things.

When Linda hadn't come back by eleven, he began to worry. Then he got mad. She had no right to do this to him, not when he was the one whose reputation was on the line. But after he called a few friends who said they hadn't seen her, he worried again. Maybe she was right. This whole thing had made him crazy. She would come back, and then maybe he would apologize. In the morning he would get rid of the tools and books. He would have a talk with Pelkner. He would pay for the fuel pump. He would even get to know his neighbors if necessary. The day had exhausted him. He put on his pajamas and lay in bed, waiting for Linda.

As he lay there he could not put the fuel pump out of his mind. When he closed his eyes he saw it in a glistening sheath of new grease, fed by its network of hoses, coddled by gaskets.

Twelve o'clock. One. She would come back, he thought. She just wanted him to sweat. And why not? She was right. He'd behaved childishly. He remembered the tools spread out on the rug and got up to put them away. It wouldn't do for her to stumble over them in the dark. Even here he'd been childish, buying every tool he saw. All he needed was a screwdriver and a pair of pliers, but spending money had been a way of feeding his wounded pride.

The tools lay on the rug like technological wreckage on the lunar surface. He put the socket sets back together. He ranked the screwdrivers in their clear plastic pouches. But when he lifted the flex-head ratcheting drive handle, when he felt the lethal heft of it, when its polished steel barrel caught a shred of moonlight, everything changed.

With his tools he knew he could do anything. Linda no longer mattered. Pelkner no longer mattered. Only the fuel pump, his tools, his revenge.

Feverishly, he piled the wrenches, pliers, screwdrivers, and the rest into the box, gathered it up, and went outside. The cool night breeze riffled the edges of his pajamas. It was colder than he'd thought, but when he turned back to put something warmer on, he found he'd locked himself out. It didn't matter. He looked off across the dim lawns of his neighbors. Shrubbery foamed from the borders of yards. Dogwood blossoms, luminous flakes, trembled in the breeze. He scooped up the gloves lying next to the step, dropped them into the box with the tools, and, fully armed, headed for the Volkswagen.

Gravel near the curb stung the soles of his feet, but he danced gingerly to the other side. The slight shift and clatter of his box of tools seemed unnaturally loud. He crept up the driveway and knelt before the engine. He hoped the car was older than '73. That year, he'd read, Volkswagen began using crimped metal edges as connectors instead of screws. Impossible to remove the fuel pump. But no, there it sat, a pre-'73 engine with a screwed-down fuel pump kneeling shyly behind the fan belt. He was pleased.

He quickly pried off the fuel hose and unscrewed the two nuts on the mounting stud at the flange. He loved the word so much he whispered it aloud. "Flange." Gasoline had begun to trickle from the dangling fuel hose. The craggy surface of the driveway scraped his knees. When he lifted the fuel pump clear of the engine, his pain and discomfort vanished.

He wondered if his luck was still holding as he went around the side of the car and tried the door. The latch popped and the door sprang open as if by itself. He released the hand brake and carefully guided the car backward down the steep driveway. The farther down he maneuvered it, the heavier it became. When he couldn't hold it any longer, he leaped clear, the open door swiping his right foot. The car scudded down the driveway, over the corner of the lawn, and followed an arc across the empty street until the back tires butted against the curb.

He lay on the lawn where he'd fallen, listening, but no one seemed to have heard the runaway car. His foot throbbed painfully. He took a few deep breaths. He shifted his weight so he lay on one hip, the cotton pajamas no protection against the sharp grass.

When the pain in his foot subsided, he limped to the car and pushed it down the sloping street. At the end the pavement ran out into an empty lot overgrown with tall weeds. He pushed the car as far into the field as he could manage. The tall weeds rustled against the sides and cracked under the tires. When he finished, he followed the dotted line of gasoline back up the street and up the driveway. At the top, on the oil-stained floor of the carport, he laid the greasy gloves next to each other. He placed the fuel pump in their upturned palms.

His revenge was complete. He would give anything to see her face next morning.

But the quiet made him wonder if he'd fallen into a trap. What if she was sitting at her bedroom window right now?

Already dialing for a squadron of downy-cheeked policemen, her face dimly illuminated by the glow of her Princess phone? No one would believe that he was innocent. He thought of her car dripping gasoline in the overgrown field.

Edna Pelkner's backyard was bordered by tall hedges. When he stretched to his full height he could see into the neighboring yards. There was no sound on the cool breeze but the hum of air conditioners shifting through their cycles, and the occasional rustle and flap of night birds in the darkened treetops. In the next yard, water slipped noiselessly back and forth between the sides of a swimming pool. The underwater lights stared fiercely at him.

He went through the side yard, ducking under pie-tin bird feeders hanging from the limbs of two pine trees. Underneath, the ground was littered with pine needles, scattered seed, and tufts of tall grass outside the mower's reach. The uncut grass reminded him of Pelkner's husband, who died shortly after he and Linda moved into the neighborhood. If she could find a way, he thought, she'd probably blame that on me, too. He crossed under cover of the trees to the house and stopped at her bedroom window. He placed a hand on either side and stretched up to look through the partly drawn blinds. His toes pressed into the dry pine needles as he leaned forward.

At first he could see nothing. But when his eyes adjusted, he saw her lying asleep against one edge of a large bed, a light blanket drawn up to her chin.

The other side of the bed was undisturbed. Her husband's side. The pillowcase was still freshly pressed. A corner

HAVEN'T YOU EVER SEEN CARY GRANT?

of the blanket was turned back for him. Everything was arranged as if he might only be in the bathroom, or checking the stove, or bagging the trash, not dead and gone. An open book lay on the bedstand, a folded pair of reading glasses on the open page. Pale yellow light from a reading lamp filled a teacup next to the book. The light made the porcelain translucent, a glowing membrane. The light glinted on the sightless lenses of the reading glasses. It fell quietly across the empty white space beside the sleeping woman.

Everything was still. The darkness felt thick. The moon was a piece of soap. Overhead, the cold breeze groped among the tops of the pines. It blew over the green lawns gone gray in the moonlight, over the car hidden among the creaking weeds, over the fuel pump dripping like a bleeding heart.

All Along the
Watchtower

*H*IS CAR STRAINING UP THE MAIN ROAD to the prison, past a crew collecting trash, Gilroy prays that none of the eleven hundred guards, inmates, and administrators will see that his registration has run out, his possibilities have expired, his hopes decayed.

Last night, after being gone for a day and a half, his wife, Millie, checked herself into the psych ward of the county hospital. And now this job, the job he took because he thought he could make a difference, has become some kind of desperate joke.

He wants to tell Sunshine all about her leaving, about the call from the hospital, about the way the doctor spoke to him with slow, reasonable words, like a kidnapper: *We've got your wife. She's safe. Now here's what we want you to do.* Later, when he brought clothes and toiletries as instructed, they treated Gilroy like a criminal, not letting him any closer to his wife than the nurses' station.

The road crew look ridiculous in their orange plastic overalls. Circus clowns, alien cowboys. As one of them watches Gilroy's car take the last curve, the inmate next to him lifts his trash spear up high. It looks as if he might drive it straight through his partner's foot. Watching nearby, the man with the gun doesn't move.

Fairhope is a medium-security prison surrounded by farmland, in a place called Pleasant Gap. Such cheap ironies hit them all — inmates, administrators, guards — as proof of the world's bad will. Inside, every wall and ceiling, every bar and pass gate, is the pale green of cheap dinnerware. Even the heavy chairs and the podium in Gilroy's classroom have thick skins of green. Except for the guard towers mounted with machine guns, except for the double row of ten-foot fencing topped with razor wire, the prison might be mistaken for a public school.

This is what he knows about the inmates: Brown uniforms are for maintenance and the furniture shop. White for kitchen help. Green for groundskeepers and farm laborers. Three afternoons a week, Gilroy teaches a course called Culture and Values. He wears a tie and tweed.

The prisoners buy and sell each other with cigarettes, speed, and quaaludes. If they side with the power or make a sacrifice for someone, they are "thorough." If they go it alone, they get cut.

"You do it when you walk past him," Sunshine explained to him once. "Not to kill him, just as a sign. You step into his world, you know?" His empty hand flashed at Gilroy's stomach as he passed. "Quick. Like-see, like-so. And there you go with your guts hanging out."

When a prisoner wants privacy, he beats up his cellmate and gets a few days in solitary, DW, Detention Wing. When he wants a real rest, he plays the death game. He waits until he hears a guard coming, then hangs himself from an upper bar. If he times it right, he goes to the infirmary for a couple of weeks.

On the yard they huddle near the inner fence in twos and threes. They stretch their arms and slap their sides for warmth. They watch the gritty hills, they stare across the long wintry distances.

Gilroy's late for class. He's bent into the open car door, hauling his book bag out of the back seat. Someone's coming up behind him. He stuffs a stack of mints into his mouth.

"Hey, Teach, you here to hang out with your favorite spade?"

Gilroy straightens up. "Why don't you just give it a rest?"

Kozempchak. The material of bad movies. A big man who carries his gut around proudly, like a trick pig. Touch it. Go ahead. I want you to. The inmates buy their drugs from him. They go to the prostitutes he brings to the edge of the far field. Businessman, man of compassion. He's got forty pounds of ugly fun on his hip — .38 Special with ammo, tear gas grenade, handcuffs, walkie-talkie, a set of brass knuckles, and a handful of hollow-points. He once laid all these things out on a tabletop for Gilroy, a kid showing off his Christmas toys.

"And this," he said, holding up a black-enameled baton, "is my PR-23. 'PR' stands for Personal Relations, and it's twenty-three inches long." He slapped the baton against his open palm. "He's built big, like his daddy."

Now Kozempchak follows him into the guardhouse and watches while he opens his book bag and is swept with the metal detector. After the wand whoops obscenely over Gilroy's keys, over his tin of mints, Kozempchak says, "You know what really honks me?" His eyes light up. "You don't care *what* kind of slime you cozy up to. I mean, these guys are *crim*inals."

Six months at the prison have taken a toll on Gilroy. The constant fear, the constant effort to hide the fear. At the end of every day, he swims. The pool in the basement of Admin was the old warden's project for reducing prison stress. But ever since the drowning a few months ago, the inmates haven't been allowed to use it. A stabbing, actually, and then the body set adrift, floating on a plume of blood.

In fact, Gilroy's the only one who uses the pool. He loves the feeling of being buoyed up by all that water, of not having to bear his own weight, like flying in slow motion. He likes to think he comes away from every swim a new man.

Late last night, Gilroy's wife called. She'd been gone a day and a half, and he'd been telling himself not to worry, not to worry. He was sure it was her, even though all he could hear was her wet, ragged breathing. He was afraid to say anything more than hello, afraid she'd hang up. They stayed like that for a long time, without speaking. In the distance he heard chimes calling people to emergencies.

By the time Gilroy gets through the search, he's late for class. He cuts across the empty plot of ground between the front gate and the Education Wing. He breaks into a jog, his heart hammering. With every lunge, his book bag bangs against his legs. With every lunge, his plastic pocket flask jingles its little bit of bourbon. Halfway across, puffing, wheezing, he's almost grateful to be stopped by an amplified voice.

"Sir, you are in a restricted area. Stand where you are and hold your arms away from your body."

He peers up at the tower. The late-afternoon sun shines straight into his eyes. He can barely see. "You know me," he calls out. "I'm the teacher. I'm only going to class."

"Walk back the way you came, slowly, holding your arms away from your body." Gilroy sees the guard set the bullhorn down, hears the slick click of a gun bolt being drawn, sees him bring the butt of his M-16 to his shoulder. With the dark mouth of his gun, the guard leads him off the grass. Gilroy's scared. He takes long, delicate strides back to where he began, arms outstretched, book bag dangling painfully from one curled hand. He feels like an ancient flying machine being wheeled toward an impossible edge.

When he bursts into the Education Wing, he nearly trips over his students, who are sitting on the hallway floor, their backs against the walls, their legs stretched out across the floor, putting themselves in the way. Here any exercise of power has significance, every measure of freedom matters.

As they climb slowly to their feet and walk into the room, someone says, "You're late," a guy they call Johnny Three-Go. He's never said a word before now. Gilroy feels like ripping his head off and squeezing out all his vital resources. Instead, he smiles.

As Gilroy starts to teach — *For what crime was Socrates imprisoned?* — Kozempchak takes his place in the hall. Protector, preserver of Gilroy's life. The wall is a solid sheet of reinforced glass. "For your protection," the warden said. Outside, Kozempchak's blue back flattens against the glass. For protection.

Inside, they talk. Sunshine, Mokey, Lewis, Sprague, and a few M&M's like Johnny Three-Go, who hardly ever speak — the Mostly Medicated. The others love to talk and smoke, leaning on their spread knees, spent cigarettes piling up at their feet. Justice, pride, and revenge are the constant topics. Gilroy fills the silences with his own words. They let him. They think he likes it. He lets them.

After a while, they take a break from Socrates and his problems. In the hall the inmates stand or squat on their heels like farmers in a field. Kozempchak moves to the end of the hall, where he can get a clear bead if anything should happen. His hand rests on his holstered gun. Lightly, hopefully.

"I can relate to that Socrates," Sunshine says as he lights up, "but why didn't he break out when he got the chance is what I want to know." Sunshine's name comes from his job, tending the prison greenhouse. His real name is Melvin, "as in . . . and the Bluenotes." He's a small man with a hook-shaped scar on his upper lip. From a fishing accident, he says. But Gilroy's heard it was a gang thing.

"I wouldn't mind dying," Sprague says. Middle-aged, thinning hair, in for a money crime. His injured gaze turns from one face to another. "I prefer death to the shame of incarceration."

"Bullshit," Sunshine says. He has no patience for Sprague, who's always pointing out that he doesn't belong with *real* criminals. He points his lit cigarette at Sprague. "That what you really want, white boy? To die?"

Sprague sighs heavily. "I can't say I don't."

"Because lots of guys in here'd do you for free. You're looking at one."

Sprague jumps to his feet and backs toward Kozempchak.

A few inmates laugh. One yells, "I'll do you, Sprague!" Another, "No, let me!"

"You animals stay away from me!"

Sunshine blows smoke. "That guy's dumb as ditch water." Sprague stays with Kozempchak for the rest of the break.

As the others go back into class, Sunshine says, "By the way, I put up your name. When we riot we're going to let you be the hostage. I told the brothers you'll be nice and quiet and read a book or something."

"Call my secretary," Gilroy says. "See if I have any open days on my calendar."

When Sunshine smiles, you can see every square inch of his gums. When he smiles, the pink knob of scar tissue on his upper lip spreads out flat and glossy. "Go ahead. Joke. But you might like it. We'll hip you to the jail's-eye view of things."

Gilroy glances quickly down the hall, where Sprague's still whimpering about "animals." He whispers, "You're not really going to riot, are you?"

Sunshine looks away.

"It's all right," he says, shaking him lightly by the sleeve. "You can talk to me. We can talk."

"You want to talk?" Sunshine says, suddenly serious, slowly detaching the hand from his sleeve. "Tell me about your old lady."

"What?"

"How many times a night she like it? How many ways?" And then, to Gilroy's stung face, "Yeah, you want to talk." He drops his cigarette, the glowing end shattering softly on the floor.

From the end of the hall, Kozempchak yells, "What are you two mooks talking about?"

"Greek philosophy," Gilroy says as Sunshine heads into the classroom. "We're talking about Socrates."

"Right. I never did trust teachers and books."

"I can tell."

Then Kozempchak, booming: "You know how fast I can have your ass behind bars? You know how little it takes? You're *that* close, my friend." Sprague, next to him, nodding.

It's what Gilroy wants more than anything. A little privacy in DW, a real rest in the infirmary.

The last of the M&M's wanders back to class. Johnny Three-Go.

"You were late," he says from his slack, smiling face.

Gilroy feels his head start to swell. He'd like a little swallow of bourbon. He leans in close. Slowly, carefully, he whispers, "Fuck you."

Sometimes Gilroy tells himself that Millie wouldn't be where she is if she didn't have such an old-fashioned name. Millie. It makes you think of gingham dresses and church suppers, pies cooling in kitchen windows.

Her doctor says she's suicidal, but Gilroy wonders how that can be. Don't you have to try to kill yourself to be called suicidal? Does it mean you're suicidal when all you do is spend a lot of time sitting in the car? Does it mean you're suicidal if you just can't stand being touched anymore? Gilroy can't figure it out. Wanting not to be alive — that's something everybody feels sometimes, isn't it?

Later, after class, after Kozempchak herds the inmates away, Gilroy sits at one of the desks to grade the papers he's just collected. *Tell about the most important moment in your life.* Most of the essays begin with variations on the same theme: *"Guilty!" the judge said as he slammed his gavel down.* One's about the Raiders' move to L.A. Another, obviously plagiarized, is about designer drugs, many of its sentences beginning, *Our own lab studies have shown. . . .*

Sunshine has written a detailed account of his wedding day, the wedding he hopes to have someday. The first sentence reads, *When I close my eyes, I see camellias.*

But mainly Gilroy reads about crime, about the look in a victim's eye, about betrayal and guilt, about the glory of a well-oiled gun. When he's finished, he feels dirty. It's been a long day. He needs a swim.

The sun has dropped behind the frozen hills. On his way to Admin, he passes A-block, the cell block for the well-behaved. And stops. Usually Sunshine's watching from his window, but not today. Pale light edges between the bars, enlarging the night. Gilroy can see a piece of string slung corner-to-corner, like a clothesline. Clipped to it are photographs too small to see clearly from where he stands.

He crosses the dead grass, waiting for the sound of the guard's bullhorn, the gun bolt's click. As he walks toward the window, he can see the pictures more clearly. A little girl in tight braids. An old man sitting in front of a birthday cake. A woman in Lycra, dancing. Others.

As he gets closer to the window, he decides to tell Sunshine about the most important moment in his own life. He'll show him they can talk. A moment that slipped right past him. How the night before Millie left, he woke up to find her crying quietly beside him. Saying, *The wind is telling me things.* Saying, *Don't make me go near the window.* How he said nothing, just gave her a hard look and said nothing. And wasn't this — his eyes closing, his body turning again toward sleep — a kind of murder?

He turns to see a green ambulance being waved inside the gate. That's why the tower guard hasn't tried to stop him. Everyone's watching it roll slowly toward A-block, cold gravel popping under its heavy tires.

And then he's standing at the lighted square of Sunshine's window. And then he sees.

"Step away, sir! Step away from the window!"

Can't I just see her for a minute?
That would be inadvisable.
But I'm her husband.
Yes.

Gilroy badly needs to swim. He needs the pure blue window of water beneath him. The clear liquid thickness of it. But the water's been murky and green since the pumps and filters were shut off after the stabbing. Like swimming through syrup. The pool's divided in half by a pontoon bulkhead where an armed guard used to patrol. A piece of it has fallen off. Over the months it's been sliding slowly to the deepest part of the pool. A square shadow under the diving board.

Soon he's lost in the laps, in the slap and kick of his passage. The lane lines on the bottom of the pool are distant, twisting shadows. He stays on course by keeping an eye on the black chunk of bulkhead far below.

The water's cold. After thirty lengths, his neck muscles stiffen painfully. His shoulders ache with every twisting plunge. Chlorine stings his eyes, his sinuses. On the turns, he has trouble fighting through his own wake.

Sunshine was already dead when Gilroy looked into his window. A heap on the floor. Kozempchak, standing outside the cell, was smiling down at the body. He looked as if he'd been standing there a long time, just enjoying the show. When he saw Gilroy, he waved, his face creasing with serene malice.

Word is that Sunshine was only playing the death game. When he heard the guard's footsteps, he slipped on his headphones, knotted the cord around his neck, and plugged into his stereo. Hendrix. He was listening to Hendrix. When the footsteps were right outside his cell, he yanked the cord tight and waited. Before he blacked out, Kozempchak probably showed himself, complaining to the dying man about the cold, knocking ice from his boots with his baton, singing snatches of country songs. Sunshine probably knew then how things would go.

Gilroy saw the bloody gouges on his neck where he'd tried to claw the knot loose, Hendrix wailing hotly in his ears. But the plastic cord was soft. The knot just melted into itself. He probably hissed curses at Kozempchak and the knotted cord around his neck, his tongue a swollen blue muscle in his mouth. Kozempchak wouldn't save anyone.

Exhausted, Gilroy hangs on to the slop channel for a minute before pulling himself out. But the door bangs open, and Kozempchak comes swaggering to the edge of the pool. He leans on his knees, gun belt creaking. "You a good swimmer, Teach?"

"No," Gilroy says, "not good." He tries to climb out of

the pool, but Kozempchak squats down at the edge, putting himself in the way.

He smells of cigarettes. His eyelids are puffy and yellow. "You want to know what I hate more than anything? Paperwork. People can blow a little thing like this" — he waves his hand vaguely — "all out of proportion, and you're up to your neck in paperwork."

Gilroy shivers. The water's cold. Icy. "I saw you," he says. "You just stood there and watched him die."

Kozempchak squats down, shakes his head. "Something's always dying around here. Don't you know that by now? And anyway, what's important is what you did not see. You did not see me lay a hand on that nappy head. Point of fact, your little friend was a victim of Sudden In-Custody Death Syndrome. Happens all the time. And anyway, what really *did* you see? Not much." He shakes his head. "Not so fucking much."

"I know what I saw."

Kozempchak slides his baton free and leans on it with both hands, a third leg. "Hell, I helped you out. You don't know who your friends are. This is a rough place. Something could happen to you. Something was going to happen." He looks out over the water. "You remember that fellow they found dead in here?"

"Are you threatening me?"

"You remember."

Gilroy pushes himself a few feet away from the edge, treading so clumsily he keeps slapping water into his face.

"I'm not finished with you, my friend." Kozempchak

raises his baton and gives the water a hard chop. "You listening? If you're not careful, things are going to get real western around here."

Gilroy dives toward the deepest part of the pool. His neck muscles cramp. His head aches. Every heartbeat is a spasm. When he touches bottom, his lungs are burning. He doesn't care. He grabs hold of the heavy bulkhead to anchor himself. It's like a rubber radiator. I'll stay down here forever if I have to, he thinks, looking up through the thick water. At the trembling blue uniform. At the baton chopping, chopping.

This Is the Last
of the Nice

I AM A MAN OF MILD MANNER. BUT lately I've been a little unwell, a little punk, a little — you know — crazy. Not Patsy Cline crazy. Not thrill-kill crazy. Just crazy crazy. Hell, I don't hang from a flagpole forty stories up, or anything close. What I am is tired. Very, very tired. It's the economy. It's the greenhouse effect. It's the millennium. But it sure the hell isn't me.

The big plate-glass window in the hospital lobby, with its black miniblinds slicing up the scenery, that would make anyone nervous, right? And the dangerous revolving door. And the hallway at one end of the room leading to the real hospital, the hallway at this end leading to my destination, the mental health center, Club Cuckoo. Who wouldn't feel a little off his feed?

My miseries are so ordinary. I'm a cold caller for an insurance company, reminding the elderly that they're more prone to robbery, disease, and accidents than the rest of us. But I don't want to talk about that. And my wife ran off three weeks ago, but I don't even want to think about that. Up to then we were always together. Ned and Naomi, like a team of draft horses.

It was supposed to be nothing more than another white-water vacation with her women's group. She'd go off with them once in a while, down the Colorado, the American. But this last time she decided never to come back. Just like that. She let me know by postcard. *I can't come back.* That's all she wrote. I laughed when I read it. It was like some wild river had finally gotten the better of her, and now she and her raft were too lost to find the way home. But it wasn't a joke. Well, let that go. Let it go.

Across from me sits a large woman, asleep, an oxygen tank pumping and hissing at her feet. Her face inflates and deflates with each wet breath. Her limp blond hair has a greenish tint. The clear tube hooked over her ears and under her nose looks like a necklace that won't fit.

Another woman, younger and almost as heavy, sits next to me. Her hair came out of the same bottle. A two-year-old totters back and forth between them. She's wearing purple tights and a red and yellow striped shirt. It's so short it shows her soccer-ball belly. And those legs. She collapses against her mother and breaks into hoarse laughter.

The mother tickles her under the chin. "Annie-fanny funny-face!" The baby giggles. Her hands are bright red, as if they've been dipped in gore. When the mother sees me looking, she says, "Finger paint." She catches a hand and picks off a few flakes while the baby tries to wriggle away. "Didn't have time to wash up after Lotta Tots, did we, Annie-fanny?" The baby flashes her greasy grin and rubs her face on

108

her mother's knee, which is as large as a throw pillow, then breaks free and hobbles over to Grandma.

The mother glances outside at the pale blue sky shredded with dark clouds, like smoke from some catastrophe, and says, "Weather coming." She peels her hair away from her face and drapes it behind her ears. "Looks like the last of the nice." The horizon is shaggy with dark clouds. They're coming closer. Grandma's sleeping with her back to the weather. How can she do that? It's the most frightening thing I've ever seen. The woman asleep and the weather coming, coming.

"Yessir," the younger woman says, "it's supposed to get cold as old Sam Scratch. They already got six inches in the panhandle."

I hate it when Nebraskans describe the western reach of the state like that. Panhandle. More like a stump. I screw up my mouth to let her know this.

"Almanac's promising the hardest winter in twenty years." She shakes her head. "Only September and already a killing frost. Now, I ask you — is that fair?"

Overnight, the flowers have blackened in their beds. The leaves of the young dogwood are black at the tips. They don't know they're already dead. I say it out loud: "The dying has begun."

The woman's eyes tick to my face. She gives me a wide broken smile. "Well, that's one way to put it."

It's the only way. The birds know it, weighing down the branches of the dogwood. They're distraught, they're over the edge, they're pissed. The wind is gusting twenty miles an hour, and everything's bugging them. The sound of their outrage seeps through the thick hospital glass. They're flapping and shrieking. They can't sit still. They want to pull the spindly tree clear out of the ground. Never speak your heart. Never.

But the only thing that really worries me, the only thing that kind of ties my knickers in a knot, is the feeling I get once in a while that if I turn my head too fast I'll flip ass-over-teakettle straight across the cosmos. But that's pretty common, wouldn't you say? Everybody feels like that, right? Lucky for me, I'm prepared for every eventuality. I figure the angles. I know the degrees of freedom. I look sharp. I stand clear. I am, after all, an insurance man.

And don't get me wrong — sleeping in the closet, that isn't a regular thing with me. It's silly, but I like the dark. And besides, it's bigger than you think. My only regret is telling the therapist. I admitted that sometimes the day is stacked against me so, I don't even come out. But I'm not worried. I'll be fine. I think maybe there's something wrong with my diet.

It's my job to point out how many ways the world can kill and maim. We have coverage for all of it. We're especially generous for dismemberment, which is so much worse in the imagination than death. "You live on a farm, Mrs. Hinkle? With machinery?" Mostly they hang up. Sometimes a word or two is enough to sell them — *combine, thresher.* Sometimes a lie. I'm a messenger bringing the bad news that hasn't happened yet.

She catches me staring. "You're looking at those little bow-legs on Annie?" It's true. The baby is the bowleggedest thing I've ever seen. "We're here to have those legs all broke so she can walk straight. Go on, Annie, go get on Grandma. Snatch her oxygen tube!" The baby runs to her grandmother. It's like watching a pair of pliers run. She pulls herself up the side of Grandma. Her crooked legs seem built for climbing. When she's high enough, she snatches at the tube.

Grandma snorts awake and bats playfully at Annie. Her nervous laugh crumbles into a volcanic cough. Tectonic plates are bucking. The crust is cracking. Magma is surging. I hook my foot around the leg of my chair.

"Now punch her," the mother says. "Punch Grandma!" The baby delivers several body blows before the grandmother, gasping, can pry her off and lower her to the floor.

A week after Naomi left, I got another card: *You deserve the truth — I have fallen in love with Buddy, our raftmaster. Please be happy for me.* And a few days later, another: *I'm so crazy in love I won't even come home for my clothes.* Just let it go, I tell you. Think about something else. The sign at my end of the lobby:

ST. REGIS

MENTAL HEALTH CENTER

AND

ADDICTION RECOVERY CENTER

Up and down, the words read: "Mental Addiction" (yes), "Health and Recovery" (you wish), "Center Center" (what the hell is that?). Try the words in different combinations: "Mental Recovery," "Health Addiction." I want a message. I want a witness. I want a drink. I want, very badly, to beat the living shit out of something. I do not want to go through this embarrassing group-therapy nonsense.

As if she's heard my thought, my therapist appears in the corner of my eye, gliding across my retina and out the door in the far wall. I let my gaze go slack so I won't have to exchange looks with her, but still I can feel the heavy drag of her eyes over my face.

I've been seeing her for a couple of months. Janet, call me Janet. A tall woman in her late forties who has a habit of screwing up her mouth when she wants to show she's unhappy with something you've said. It's where I picked up the habit. I'm trying it out. It hurts my mouth muscles. Like French. And besides, I have very few honest opportunities to make the gesture. Nothing much bothers me. Not really. Sometimes at night the line of light under the closet door. But I can stuff a towel into it and make the darkness complete. What I like is to make it so dark there's no difference between my eyes open and my eyes shut. What I like is to take in the faint scent of Naomi still clinging to her clothes — sharp as ozone, tender as sin.

It bothers me sometimes the way Janet talks as if there are several people inside me all fighting to get out, monkeys in a cage. "Not *that* one," she'll say. "I don't want to talk to the *nice* one. I want to do battle with the *mean* one."

The first time she said it, I said, "The mean one wants to know if we can get a group rate for these sessions."

She made her mouth, a demented kiss. I remember thinking, We are not getting out of this alive.

It's true I have a bit of a crush on her. Not much. I'm being very professional about this. Hell, you can like your

therapist, can't you? Without it being all Freudian and everything? I like the way she reacts sometimes to my stories about
my father — the time he locked me naked outside the house,
the time he tied me to the toilet. Ordinary extremities. "Son
of a bitch!" she says, nearly jumping out of her chair. I don't
tell the stories to learn anything about myself. What's the
point? Such a long time ago. I only want to entertain her. But
what happens when I run out of stories? I'll lie, of course.

"Where is it?" she said yesterday. "Your rage?" She
handed me a piece of construction paper and a box of
crayons. "Draw me a picture of your rage." I stared at the
blank sheet for a long time and then, before I knew what I
was doing, I tore it into careful squares, smaller squares,
smaller yet. "I don't have any rage," I said, letting the paper
dust fall from my hands.

"I'd like you to consider joining a group I'm putting
together." She scratched a comment on her clipboard. "It's a
Men's Post-Traumatic Stress Disorders Group."

"But I wasn't *in* Vietnam."

She stopped writing and looked up. "There's all kinds of
wars out there."

The group room is strange. I expected the molded plastic
chairs set in a circle, but not the totem pole made from
papier-mâché and tinsel, or the brightly colored drawings
pinned to the wall. Despite these efforts to brighten the
room, I can feel it, the leftover sadness, like a smell.

My therapist is making coffee. She's wearing a calf-length
blue dress with a design of small white flowers no bigger than

gnats. Very matronly. She knows my mind. On each drawing is a name painted in sparkles, a few words crayoned under it. "RON — that I have nice hands." "SUSAN — that I have a nice car." "CHAZ — that I'm good in sorry."

"Do you run a group for kids?" I'm trying to be nice, right?

Janet shakes her head. "That's our wall of pride. They were done by children, yes, but not the kind you're thinking of." She points at the long wall, from which three blank sheets of butcher paper hang ceiling-to-floor. "After a few weeks, you and the others will fill this wall with your own words and pictures."

It's all I can do to turn my back on the blank wall and sit in the circle. Next to the pride pictures is a window looking across the garden to the other wing. The blinds of the window opposite are partly drawn, but I can see the silhouette of a man pacing, his head shifting mournfully from side to side.

I've been afflicted with tests, the most cruelly named of which is the SCIDS test. It's a measure of how dissociated I am, that is, *we* are. "Do you talk to your appliances?" (Only when they get out of line.) "Do you talk to yourself?" (Exactly which one of us are you addressing?) "Have you made a real commitment to therapy?" (I'm here, right?) "Does it ever seem to you as if you do things against your better judgment?" (I'm here, right?) When the test-giver stopped looking me in the eye, I knew I was flunking with flying colors.

Next, in the dismal way my luck runs, I flunked Prozac.

They started me on twenty milligrams a day, then upped it to forty. After three weeks, there seemed to be no effect. Secretly I raised my dose to sixty, but without results. They promised me an oceanic high. They promised me days filled with sunlight and grace. But after six weeks, everything still tasted like cardboard.

A tall thin man comes into the room and perches on the chair across the circle. Neatly trimmed black hair and a mustache so delicate he probably has to feed it with an eyedropper. His name, he says quietly, is Alston. He makes his living developing computer games. "I was the principal designer of Lunatics at Large." His eyes go out of focus. "There was a time when I thought that was funny."

Bill, who comes in next, has a rugged face and closely cropped hair. He supports himself as a freelance referee for high school basketball and football games. He has big blocky hands, hands that like to signal penalties. I wedge my own hands under my thighs.

"Ned," I say. "I own a bar on the west side."

Janet shoots me a look.

"More of a nightclub, really."

Things are off to a bad start. It's junior high. We're backed up against the gym wall, knowing we'll never get invited to dance. We sit there for a few minutes, smiling dumbly. Then the coffeepot wheezes itself full, and we make a big show of helping ourselves, grateful for something to do.

When we're seated again and sipping, Janet says, "Bill, how about you? You've been through the routine before.

Maybe you can get us started. What brings you here this time?"

Bill's face struggles for words. He squares off his idea with those hands, planes it flat, turns it back and forth.

"All right," he says, "OK." He acts like Janet's beaten a confession out of him, which is what a lot of my sessions with her are like. "You want to know about pain? About hurt?" He looks at us with frightened eyes.

I say, "What do you think we're going to say — 'Thank you, Bill, but we're not interested in your pain'? Go for it. Let's get this over with." Janet's eyes have turned to stone.

I am immune. I have no feelings. It's the one thing I thank my father for. Someday, from her cellular phone, just as her dinghy goes twisting over the falls, Naomi will ask for forgiveness. But even then, there will be nothing on my heart's oscilloscope but a dead-even line. Farewell, my love. *Bon voyage.*

Bill says, "OK." He says, "All right. I play in an adult softball league. I don't know how much you know about the game, but I'm batting and the count is three-and-oh. I'm supposed to take, right? I mean, *I* know this. But can I help it when a fat pitch comes right down the line? I go for it, right? I miss, of course. And miss. And miss again. Back in the dugout, the guys are on me: 'What're you doing, going on a three-and-oh? You're supposed to take!' Man, that hurt."

"That's it?" I say. "Are you kidding?"

Janet ignores me and looks at Alston, nodding slowly. "Sound familiar?" Alston smiles and nods back at her. I feel a surprising stab of jealousy. I've let myself think I'm Janet's only patient. Client. Client. I don't like the thought that she spends time with others, listening to their stories, stories that might be better than mine. From now on I'll lie. Dream up some tale of woe to make this guy's pain seem like so much pocket fluff.

Janet has to say it twice before I hear her. "What about you?" It's her great talent — timing.

"I'm not interested in sports," I say.

"That's not what I mean."

Pity. On all their faces. Pity. "Am I the only one who doesn't want to be here?"

"Talk about that," Janet says.

"I feel fine," I say. "I just get a little edgy now and then." A nerve in my eyelid is twanging. Can she see it? Stop it. Stop it.

Janet can be very mean when she wants to be, and it looks like she wants to be. She folds her hands in her lap and sets her head. "Why don't you tell us about that deathtrap you drive?" She smiles like a movie villain.

My turn to make a mouth. I drive a Pinto — orange with black interior — I bought for five dollars. Worth every penny. I hung a pair of fuzzy dice from the mirror and set about driving it into the ground. Things keep going wrong. Headlights burn out two months after I put them in. The exhaust pumps thick white smoke. Every time I use the heater, water drips onto the floor. And of course at every stoplight I wait for the rear-end collision that will turn me into Detroit flambé. But the damned thing just won't die.

"My wife left me," I say. "That's why I'm out of sorts. It's as simple as that. You want to dig through my past. You want me to get in touch with my feelings, my hidden motives. But all I want to know is how to deal with this." I fish out Naomi's last postcard, the one from Mexico. Uncrumple it. Show the front, a picture of an Aztec temple. Read it. Just read it. *"You haven't lived until you've DONE IT on an altar where hundreds of virgins were sacrificed!* What are you supposed to do when your wife sends you a card like this? That's what I want to know. That's all I want to know."

A silence blank as butcher paper. Then Janet says, "That isn't what she wrote, is it, Ned."

"What do you know about it?" I stuff the card into my pocket. *I'm tired of the way you let me take responsibility for your happiness. I'm tired of feeling alone in my own house. How can I come back to that?*

Alston says, "I've never even *been* to Mexico. I've never been *any*where."

"Let's stay on task, gentlemen," Janet says.

Bill's hands fly out, and he says, "Ned, what is it you want from us?"

I give him my dead-level voice. "I want you to shut up, Bill. And I want you to sit on those hands."

Janet looks at me as if I've derailed the entire recovery movement.

I say, "You think I'm out of my head. Is that it?"

"No," she says very carefully, "but I think that's where you'd like to be."

"I don't have to sit still for this." Get up. Stop shaking. "I'm hardly like *that* basket case." Point at the window, at the inconsolable silhouette passing in the far hall. "I mean, I'm hardly some kind of drooling catatonic subspecimen, would you say?"

Janet claps. "There he is — the mean one!" She holds out her hands and claws the air. "Come on," she says. "We're ready for you."

Go home. You kept your promise. You came. The silhouette moves sorrowfully past the window. "This farce is over." I turn to go. Synchronous as trained seals, the grouplings bark, "Talk before you walk!" I'm halfway out the door when Janet touches my sleeve. There it is, the mouth. I've flunked group. That's all right. I'm prepared for her, for any kind of pleading. I want to be gone, far away from here, far away from phones and mailboxes, far away from everything. I want to be somewhere in the dark, in a room so small I can't fall down.

She looks into my eyes. "Are you safe?" It's the most intimate thing anyone's ever said to me. "Are you?" she says, pulling lightly on the sleeve of my jacket.

For a second . . . for a second . . . but then I regain myself. I whisper so as not to disturb the swift recovery of the group. "The world is full of danger," I say. "*No*body's safe. Don't you know that by now?"

Outside the room, I feel as if the back of my head has floated open. Ten minutes. That's all I could take of group. I'm already embarrassed by the sorry spectacle of my rage, the untamed thing of me. But then I get an idea. I head down the hall toward the other wing. I'm going to save a soul the old-fashioned way. I'm going to shake the life back into that silhouette. No sorrow is so deep that a good, hard slap won't put you right. Right? But when I round the corner, there is no silhouette, only a maintenance man pushing a floor buffer, guiding it carefully back and forth, side to side.

"Yeah?" he says, shutting off his machine and dialing down the opera on his cassette player. "Can I help you?"

Turn slowly. Walk back down the hall, toward the angry birds, toward the dangerous world.

Right before Naomi left, I went to Kansas City for a two-day insurance seminar. When I got back I said, "Did you miss me?" "No," she said, "actually, I didn't." And it wasn't her words so much that scared me as the touch of surprise in her voice. She was already gone.

I never got mad. I never had a wild hair. I never developed unforgivable appetites or quirky habits or ungovernable interests. But I never woke her up at two in the morning with my mouth on her mouth, my hand on her breast. What I did was keep to the wall, stay out of the way. I thought that's how it was done. In the end, living with me, she said, was like living with no one at all. Can't win. Either there are too many people inside or too few.

Death and dismemberment. All the world's dangers. I sold Naomi without a word. Made her feel how little there is to trust. A chemical in the brain dries up, and you're no longer in love, can't imagine being in love. Toward the end she followed me from room to room, waiting for the words that would make sense of everything. I couldn't get away from her. I only wanted to be left alone. One day I got my wish.

*   *   *

Grandma has fallen asleep again, the respirator pumping softly at her feet, her loyal pet. The daughter is throwing dark looks her way and yanking through a magazine.

Annie, the bowlegged toddler, pliers over to me. She looks up into my eyes. I stare back at her. In a voice too deep for a baby, she yells, "Hey!" She holds out one bent leg, then the other. "Hey!" Her voice is raw, like she's been standing naked in the cold, screaming at a locked door for hours. It's the voice of someone who's about to say, Everybody suffers, everything hurts, get over it. Then she squats down and crows, "See? See? Shoes!" I look. They're brand-new, her shoes, red as ripe apples, shiny as silver.

The bad weather is closing in. Big dark rollers tumbling like bodies through deep water. As I watch, a stiff wind crosses the parking lot. The dogwood throws up its arms, leaves flying, wings flapping. What makes someone buy new shoes for a baby whose legs are about to be broken? I swear the birds are pulling the tree straight out of the ground. I want it. More than anything. But the birds settle, the branches relax, the tender leaves go limp, and everything falls strangely still. This is the last of the nice. The count is three-and-oh. You're supposed to take.

Dreamers

My wife, Christine, is a lucid dreamer. She wills her dreams. Each night before bed she chooses a place to visit or a character she'd like to meet. Sometimes it's a sensation. She dreams of diving for pearls in the South Pacific, of meeting Billy the Kid, of the color blue. My own dreams are full of tired fun-house tricks — winding staircases, dead-end passages, ghostly figures gliding just out of view.

When Lizzie, our five-year-old, can't sleep, she says, "Mommy, tell about the dream people." She loves hearing about the wise and friendly guardians of her mother's dreams. In an African village, a shaman opens his hand to show her the eye drawn on his palm. On a Greek island, an old woman gives her a wicker basket filled with song. A bird with a human voice leads her up a Peruvian mountainside to the waters of healing. In my dreams, creatures keep trying to grab me. People, too.

More than any other, Christine loves her flying dreams. The night sky above her, all around her, sharpening its edges against the stars. The clouds breaking up. Her stomach dropping. And below her the cities glittering like sea foam against the darkness.

This morning she looks especially tired. Her eyes are puffy, her cheeks creased with sleep. We're working on our first cup, both of us staring at the overgrown spider plant hanging in the kitchen window. It makes me think of Lizzie's knitting project sitting untouched on her doll shelf. I'm glad to be drinking coffee with my wife, the whole weekend stretched out in front of us.

These days I pretty much go from one meaningless job to another, waiting for something to happen. I've just finished my first week at Penney's, forty hours on my knees. I never pictured myself as a shoe salesman, but I don't guess a lot of people do.

Christine holds the rim of her coffee mug to her mouth but doesn't drink, letting the steam warm her face. She closes her eyes and smiles.

"Last night," she says, "I decided to take a lover."

Outside, cold light spills from the swollen, gray sky, but no rain.

"A dream lover," she says. She's wearing what she always sleeps in — a black sleeveless T-shirt, black panties, and white athletic socks. She rubs her lower lip along the edge of her mug in a way that I find indecent and exciting.

"A *dream* lover," I say.

"A Victorian solicitor. His name is Sebastian."

I try to smile. "As long as he's not from the neighborhood," I say.

Christine's look is cold. She's very serious about her dreams.

The lights in her eyes go out as she remembers her way back into the dream.

"His office was so glossy — all mahogany and brass. There were bookshelves everywhere, and so many law books the smell of leather made me dizzy. He smoked a pipe. From his window I could see a harbor full of ships at anchor, three-masted schooners swarming with gulls."

"And where was this solicitor?"

She smiles. "He was sitting behind his desk, watching me. I sat across from him in a lace gown. He said he knew I had come from the other world. We talked for a long time. We took tea. In the end I gave myself to him." She touches her neck. She says, "Sebastian." The name floats on a warm breath. "It was more than real."

"The truth is," I say, "I never really quite believe in your dreams."

Christine's face becomes more angular, paler. One side of her mouth hitches up a little. She looks at me as though she's caught me stealing from her.

"I'm hungry," I say, getting up from the table.

I go to the refrigerator and hang in the open door to see if there's anything to eat. Christine comes up behind me.

Without turning around, I say, "You know that old superstition? Tell your dreams before breakfast and they come true."

The frosty air falls around our feet. "Don't be silly," she says. "We never eat breakfast."

"My point," I say.

Inside the refrigerator are glass jars and plastic packages

125

filled with strange grains, liquids, and curds of protein. Weeks ago, months really, I decided our diet needed help. I dragged Christine to a natural foods store. We'll make it a project, I said. We'll learn new things. We bought the strangest food we could find. Black food. Blue food. Food with unpronounceable names. We bought everything. I thought we'd make exotic dinners for our friends. I thought with the right food we'd live forever. We brought it all home and carefully put it away. Now we never touch it except to move it aside when we're looking for the eggs, the mayonnaise.

"There's nothing to eat in here," I say.

"We can eat in the city, when we take my painting to the gallery."

"That's today? Anyway, I'm hungry now."

"None of that stuff is edible anymore." She looks deep into the refrigerator. "It's a Japanese horror movie in there."

"Lizzie and I will eat something at the mall," I say, letting the refrigerator door close.

"We'll eat in the city," Christine says.

This afternoon we're supposed to deliver Christine's latest painting to a South-of-Market gallery. We both studied art in college, but she stayed with it, and now a few of her things are beginning to sell. I don't like this one — a big canvas slashed with bright colors laid on with a jagged piece of wood. She found the wood while we were hiking at Big Basin. We came across a redwood that had been sliced open by a stroke of lightning. She tore the wood from the blasted heart of the tree. On the drive home she made me stop so she could pick up a dead rabbit she saw beside the road. And now, in the lower right corner of the canvas, she has somehow attached the rabbit skin. Thick gouts of paint run over it like gore.

When I pour her another cup of coffee, Christine says, "Have you noticed how the raccoon never comes around anymore? I hope nothing's happened to him."

He used to come by almost every morning, but the plate of scraps we put out has sat there untouched for weeks now.

I say, "The deck is so full of dry rot he's probably afraid to climb up here." This makes me think of all the other repairs I've been putting off: the doors that need planing, the paint peeling in the bathroom, the hole in the bedroom wall.

"Do raccoons hibernate? I think they do," Christine says.

"Raccoons don't hibernate," I say firmly, as if I know. "And anyway, it's only October. Something's wrong, I'm afraid."

Christine says, "Lizzie misses him. So do I. It's silly, but when I see him out there eating, I think the day is going to turn out all right." She smiles thinly. "Now I'm never quite sure."

"This place," I say, rapping the window frame, "needs major surgery."

"It'll last as long as we do," she says. And then, "You're not jealous, are you?"

"Are you kidding?" I wave her question aside, but I'm so jealous I can taste it. Jealous of her dream lover. Jealous of her hideous painting.

"I know how it sounds, but I think I'm going to be dropping in on him again." She looks down and runs her finger along the edge of the table. She looks up. "Pretty regularly, I expect."

"Sure," I say. "Why not?" My ears are burning.

"You *are* jealous."

"It's like you left our bed," I say. "It's like you slipped away for some dirty little tryst."

"It's only a dream. Harmless."

"A dream," I say slowly, ponderously, ridiculously, "is a distant cry from the buried self."

She cocks her head, her eyes squinting, as if I've told a joke she isn't getting. "Harris," she says. Maybe she means to console me, but in the still, cold air of the kitchen my name sounds like the edge of a knife.

"Have you ever noticed how your dreams never surprise you?" I say. "Have you ever noticed that? You want to make it with some guy? Poof! There he is. Just once I'd like you to have a dream that scared the crap out of you."

"You're not talking about my dreams," she says. "Let's keep things straight. You're talking about me."

"All I'm saying is, I don't see how I can trust someone who doesn't have a nightmare now and then."

Lizzie's awake. We hear the sound of her door being wrenched open. Have to remember to oil the hinges.

"That's not what you're saying, Harris. That's not at all what you're saying." She stands up suddenly, angry and shaking. She sweeps up her coffee mug and thunks it into the sink as she leaves the kitchen.

The stairs creak under her footsteps. The floorboards ache as she goes down the hall to Lizzie's room. First I hear Lizzie's sleepy cartoon mouse voice, then the rich and soothing tones of Christine's. I've placed myself beyond its reach. I sit there letting my coffee turn cold, looking out through the leggy snarl of spider plant. I want more than anything to see that raccoon come waddling out of the woods, bringing the good day back into our lives.

Prince Charles and Princess Di are dead and have to be replaced. Which is just fine, as far as Lizzie is concerned. She's raised the hamsters from nubbins, but Di was a biter and Charles had a small hairless stub instead of a right forepaw.

Lizzie's only five, but she's already an old hand with hamsters. The first few times Di bit her, she cried. After a while, though, she'd tell her off, shaking her swollen finger in the hamster's face.

Di was the first to go. One day she crawled into the corner of her cage, burrowed under the cedar shavings, and slowly faded away, so slowly that it was two days before we knew she was dead.

Charles went suddenly. On Sunday mornings, when I'm trying to sleep off my hangover, Lizzie used to creep up to our bed and put Charles on my face. I'd wake up staring into the hamster's wild red eyes. He'd stand there struggling for a foothold on my face, waving his pink stub at me. But this Sunday I woke up without Charles's help. Lizzie was standing next to the bed, crying softly. Charles had gone to hamster heaven to be with Di the biter.

So now Lizzie and I are heading to the mall to buy new

hamsters and do some errands. All the way, she chatters about them. Michael and Lisa Marie, they're to be called. The clouds are gray and close, but no rain yet.

"I hope they get married," she says, "so they'll have little pink erasers, and then I'll have a whole bunch of hamsters."

"You'll have to think up an awful lot of names," I say.

"That's easy," she says. "I'll name them after the Seven Dwarfs. But I *don't* want a Grumpy hamster. No way!"

"We'll make sure the ones we buy are nice," I say.

"That's silly, Dad," she says. "You can't tell."

"Sure you can," I say.

"You mean by seeing if they bite?"

"That's one way."

She thinks a moment, then says, "Are you going to let them chew on *your* finger?"

"What?"

"Because *I'm* not putting *my* finger in any hamster's mouth. No way! Di tasted me too many times."

I whimper melodramatically. "Don't make *me* do it. There must be another way to find the nice ones. Maybe we can just ask them a few trick questions."

"*Dad*dy!"

"You're right, you're right. They'd probably only lie to us."

Lizzie claps her hand to her forehead, closes her eyes, and shakes her head slowly.

I find a parking space next to an old Datsun sport coupe, a beautiful cream-colored car. Up close, though, I see that the body is dimpled all over from hail. Lightning flashes beyond the rim of the valley. The storm is ten or twenty miles away, moving slow. The seedlings along the bypass rock in the damp wind.

"That one looks nice," I say, pointing to a hamster in the back of the cage.

The pet store clerk, a teenager with shaggy black hair, starts to reach inside for the hamster, but then Lizzie looks closer.

"I hate to tell you, Dad, but that one looks *dead.*"

The clerk takes his hand out of the cage and says, "Whatever." He looks nervously toward the front of the store. A man stands there waiting to pay for a large hooded cat box that sits on the counter.

"No," I say, "he's just resting. He's not crazy like the others, that's all."

Lizzie rolls her eyes at me and looks back at the hamster. It does seem to be lying pretty still.

"I *know* hamsters, Dad. Trust me. This little guy is a goner." We've already chosen Lisa Marie, who's romping noisily inside the box Lizzie's holding. It's like something a Chinese dinner might come in, only with air holes.

We stare at my choice for Michael. Suddenly, its nose begins to twitch and it wriggles deeper into the shavings.

"See?" I say. "What'd I tell you? We'll take that one."

Lizzie gives me a dark look.

Michael sings a pure bleat of woe as the clerk puts him into Lizzie's box. But before he closes it, Lizzie reaches in. She inspects the hamster in her cupped hands.

"At least it's a boy." She looks up at the clerk as she puts Michael back inside the box. "If this guy dies," she says, "you owe me another hamster." At the front of the store the man hoists the cat box into his arms and walks away without paying.

The mall isn't very crowded for a Saturday. Lizzie walks with the box up near her face so she can look through an airhole at the happy couple.

We buy envelopes at the stationery store and B-complex vitamins at the drugstore. We buy two new leotards at Penney's. I keep us clear of the shoe department. I don't want someone tapping me on the shoulder, asking me to work a shift. I don't know what I'm doing at this job. I walked in one day to get some freelance sign work, window display, something that would make me feel as if I were still doing art. What they had was shoe salesman. I took it. I didn't have much choice.

Lizzie snatches a Beavis and Butt-head T-shirt from a table. "This too," she says, holding it up to herself and clamping her chin down on it.

She likes ballet class but only if she can wear a T-shirt over her leotard. She thinks she's too chubby.

I say, "Honey, you don't need that. You're beautiful."

She frowns and says, "You're my daddy. You're sup*posed* to think I'm beautiful." We buy the T-shirt.

Our last stop is the one I've been waiting for, the cable TV store. By now Michael and Lisa Marie are having a knock-down-drag-out fight, running from one end of the box to the other, scrambling and scratching around.

"It's OK," Lizzie says, peering through the airhole. "They just don't know they're married yet." Right.

We're waiting for the woman behind the counter to finish a phone call. Along one side of the shop is a bank of television screens, each tuned to a different cable station.

We see Greek gods speaking Spanish, a hitchhiker sitting on his guitar case beside a deserted highway, and a man singing "Beautiful Dreamer" while standing on a desk in nothing but polka-dot boxer shorts. I'm wondering what's on the Playboy Channel, when the woman hangs up.

"How can I help you today?" she says, turning to us. She wears her black hair pulled back from her face, but a wisp of it has come undone and curls over her right ear. I can't stop looking at it, at the delicate curve of her ear, the soft skin of her cheek.

I dig the remote control out of my jacket pocket. "My dog sort of chewed on this," I say. Lizzie looks up at me as if I've said one of the bad words. "But it still works. Look." I aim the remote at the wall of screens and press the channel selector. One of the screens jolts to another channel — a computer weather map with white electronic clouds moving in from the Pacific.

The woman frowns. She takes the remote from me and inspects the shattered corner. "Your *dog?*" she says. Her eyes are the color of motor oil.

"But it still works," I say. "I just want to exchange it."

"We'll have to send it back to the factory," she says, "to make sure it still works."

"I *told* you it works." I take it from her and snap channels again — a news team laughing and shuffling their notes, behind them a bank of television screens, a parallel universe.

"See?"

She frowns. "The changes are automatic."

Lizzie looks up at the woman and says solemnly, "We don't *have* a dog." She raises the box to eye level. "*We* have *ham*sters."

The clerk's smile is intended only for Lizzie.

"It goes back to the factory," she says to me, "and if they find out that your *dog* has destroyed it, you'll be billed for twenty-five dollars."

"Well, it still works," I say, pocketing the remote. "Let's go, Lizzie."

"Wait," Lizzie says. "Look." She holds her index finger in the air as if she were saying "Eureka!" The hamsters are smashing back and forth inside the box. She slowly puts her finger deep into one of the airholes. The commotion stops.

"I can feel them sniffing me," she whispers.

When we get home, Christine is sitting on the couch with her raincoat across her knees, waiting to go to the gallery.

I say, "We decided we weren't that hungry after walking through the food court and seeing all those people. They looked so sad, like they were being punished. Mall food." I shiver. "We couldn't eat."

Christine is smoking, using a saucer for an ashtray. I put our purchases on the coffee table so she can make sure I got the right leotards, the right envelopes, the right vitamins.

"We had an Orange Julius," Lizzie says, "and Daddy had an egg in his."

"You shouldn't tell on me," I say. "Just for that, next time I'll have them put some bacon in there with the egg."

"Yecch!" Lizzie cries and runs up to her room with her new hamsters.

"I thought you quit smoking," I say when she's gone.

"So did I," Christine says.

I sit next to her and hold out the broken remote. "They wouldn't exchange it."

"Told you."

Her painting is leaning next to the front door, wrapped in butcher paper. I'm glad I don't have to look at it.

In college the joke was that Christine and I were brought together by the Fall of the Roman Empire. We'd sit in the dark lecture hall, watching slides of crumbling friezes and fading mosaics, our hands flying out to each other like night birds. The lights always caught us by surprise, faces flushed, shirts undone. But, now that I think of it, I was the one who failed art history, not Christine.

"You still mad?" I say.

"You still jealous?"

I see her lover as a fat man with wiry muttonchops, one thumb always locked in his vest pocket, an empire builder bent on colonizing my wife. I know, in some irrational way, that historical records exist, proving that her solicitor once actually existed. Tonight I'll dream of the cable lady, naked except for a pair of red pumps.

Upstairs, Lizzie turns on her Michael Jackson tape.

Christine calls out to her, "Down, Lizzie."

"I'm still hungry," I say on my way into the kitchen.

Every time I stare into that refrigerator I feel like a scientist inspecting a failed experiment. I meant well. She can never accuse me of not meaning well.

Over the months, the food has undergone a strange mutation. The soft white brick of tofu has sprouted blossoms of blue and green mold. The dried fruit, never quite edible anyway, has hardened into tree bark. We're afraid to open the bottle of rice milk, as gray as dishwater.

Christine follows me into the kitchen and says, "Something ought to be done about that mess." She stands next to me and looks into the refrigerator. "I got a big kick out of you the day you made us buy this goop."

"I meant well," I say.

"I know," she says, "only now it's time to kill or be killed."

I say, "How do we know that's not the way it's supposed to look?"

She finds a grocery bag under the sink, gently shakes it open, and stands it on the floor in front of the dying food.

"It's time," she says.

"I guess."

With great care we place each of the strange foods in the bag, as if we think we're going to take it to some safe place and not to the trash can out back. We inspect each one before we throw it out.

"Hummus," I say.

"Kelp," she says.

"Ponzu."

"Dulse."

The mystic syllables of our love.

Go Long

*L*ITTLE BY LITTLE, MY FISH WERE CHEWING each other's faces off. Two big oscars, they hung there in the murky aquarium and stared into each other's eyes like gunslingers. One's lips were shredded. The other's brown picket of teeth stuck out through a torn square of fish flesh.

It was winter in northern California, the rainy season, and Lago Vista Villa was falling apart. There were leaks everywhere. Plaster had dropped. Two ceilings had fallen down. Complaints were turning into threats. I did what I could as manager, moving the worst to other apartments, putting the roofers on call twenty-four hours a day. But there wasn't much they could do until the rain stopped and the roofs were dry. Big flat-topped deals, each covered with a thin layer of tar paper and a few tons of gravel. Add a little rain, and you had a rooftop swimming pool.

Now, near the end of the month, the tenants committee had decided to put their rent into escrow until something was done. The mortgage payment on the complex was automat-

139

ically deducted from the bank account every month, so when all of the rent wasn't there to cover it, the owners would be fined one percent of the outstanding debt. The tenants were talking lawsuits. The owners were talking bodily harm. Mine.

I was standing in the middle of my living room, sipping a little Black Velvet, watching the oscars watch each other. Outside, a light rain sizzled in the parking lot. I was thinking I had a few full bottles of whiskey around the apartment, leftovers from various lawn parties. If I was careful, I could stay inside until spring.

That's when I saw him, across the parking lot, a big man with a jaw like a front-end loader, standing next to a blue pickup with a plywood camper built onto the back. A meat-cutter maybe. An enforcer for the mob. A man used to throwing things around. But I knew who he was, the big man blinking stupidly at me over the tops of cars. He saw me. By the time I was heading across the parking lot to him, he had broken into a grin and was waving like the deranged.

"Isn't that amazing," he said. "You knew me right off."

The rain had become steady and insistent. I didn't know what to say. I said, "You look different."

Up close I could see that all his hard edges had gone soft. Even his hair, still clipped to a quarter of an inch, now looked more like a baby's than the stiff buzz cut of a naval officer. But it was mostly his eyes that were different. Vague, watery blue.

He said, "It's been a long time." His gaze went away, as if he were trying to remember something. "Come to think of it, nothing is what it was."

Inside the camper, we sat on padded benches, a flap of

plywood folded down between us. We plucked at our damp clothes and drank strong black coffee from a large thermos.

"Good coffee," I said.

"The one absolute necessity of life." We toasted each other and drank. Then he set the thermos lid down and smiled at me. "Gee, it's good to see you."

Twenty-one years had passed. Twenty-one years, and all we could think to do was sit and stare at each other, rain chattering overhead.

"I made this camper myself," he said after a while. "Mitered every corner, beveled every edge. Feel this table." He ran his hand over the plywood leaf between us.

I slid my fingertips over the tabletop and said, "Like satin."

"Like satin," he said, nodding as if the table had not been complete until it was described in just that way.

He showed me the bunk over the cab of the truck. He pulled back a shower curtain to show me his chemical toilet. He had a propane stove and a small refrigerator that ran off an extra battery he had rigged up. He had a closet full of canned food, a spice cupboard, and a bookshelf with a handmade wooden rail that swung up to keep the books from falling out as he drove.

As he poured more coffee, he said, "I call her the Blue Norther. I swear I could live in here forever." He looked around with a sad, steady gaze as if he might have to.

We drank a lot of coffee. Outside, the rain came harder.

If my father were in an old war movie, he'd be the guy breathing live steam in the submarine's engine room. With the right wrench and a chaw, he could nurse those engines through anything the Japanese threw down. Lanky, with big square hands, he was only happy around machines, around order and efficiency. "On deck!" he'd yell each day at dawn. And if my feet didn't hit the floor fast enough, it was push-ups on the cold front porch.

My childhood was a series of close order drills. Getting dressed, eating meals, every move I made was timed and evaluated using a complicated system of merits and demerits. For a while it was like a game, but by the time I was twelve, my father had turned mean. Something had gone wrong with his life, I think, and I was the easiest explanation.

There were nights when he'd haul me out of bed and drag me outside in my underwear. "The car needs washing," he'd say. "You don't really expect me to drive to the lab in a dirty car, do you?" And he'd lecture me on cleanliness and sin with the voice that boomed across my dreams. I dragged the heavy bucket from one panel of the car to another, scrubbing it all as clean as I could manage by moonlight. After a while, this happened so often none of it seemed strange. None of it.

When the coffee ran out, we kept sitting there as if it hadn't, talking and fiddling with the cups and talking.

"You remember how I used to call you 'Sparky'?" he said.

"No," I lied. Go slow, I told myself.

We admired his camper. We talked about the blue of Monterey Bay, where he and his second wife lived. He told me about books he'd read. He gave me a recipe for 'Bama Fried Chicken. It was archaeology every inch of the way. Tooth-brushes in the dirt. Dust off a layer at a time. Don't crack the

shards. Watch for the bones. He was uncovering a lost civiliza-
tion, but so far it didn't correspond to any world I knew.

I memorized each gesture, each detail. The way his hands
lying on the table would slowly roll open as he spoke, to show
he had nothing to hide. These were the hands that flashed
through my dreams. But now they lay there helpless as
beached starfish. He wasn't my father anymore. He was just an
old guy living in a truck.

After a couple of hours, I was hungry and jittery from all
the coffee. I told him I'd throw something together for us. I
stood up and looked down at him. His hair was so short I
could see his scalp, a few brown moles. I had never seen the
top of my father's head before. He always towered over me. It
seemed like a forbidden thing to do. But he just sat there
finishing the last of his coffee, looking through the louvered
windows of his camper. I watched the strangely delicate dip of
his head to the cup. I thought of old men sitting alone at lunch
counters. Then he looked up at me.

"Coffee," he said, smiling, almost a child.

We made our way to my apartment, the air prickly with
rain. Once inside, I went straight for the refrigerator. I had to
find food. I had to feed my dad. Fruit cocktail and red onions.
Mustard. A petrified block of cream cheese. Nothing. I turned
to my father as if for advice, as if we were in a stranger's house.
Where do you think they keep the food?

We were standing in the middle of the living room. Empty
pizza boxes, dirty laundry. He stared at my chewed-up oscars
through the tea-colored water. They were floating nose-to-nose

like tethered zeppelins. One of them darted for the other, fastening its teeth onto the frayed edge of the other's mouth. They made a quick half-turn to the left, then disconnected. A small spongy bit of flesh fell softly through the water between them.

"What I need," I said, "is a drink."

We decided to go to a bar I knew downtown, but first he wanted to refill his thermos, "for later." As he scooped grounds into the coffeemaker, the phone rang.

"Mr. Boylan, this is Trooper Johns of the state police. I'm calling about your father."

"My father . . . what about him?" He slowly shoveled grounds into the coffeemaker.

"We're trying to locate him, and we're wondering if he may have contacted you."

"I would find that very strange." He measured water, pouring it carefully, quietly.

"His wife is pretty worried about him. If he tries to contact —"

"Very strange."

"But if he does, you'll contact me."

When I hung up, my father turned on the coffeemaker with obvious relief. It began wheezing and moaning, dribbling thick black dollops into the pot. We stared at it as if we had just invented it.

He said, "I had an old coon hound made a noise like that."

A sudden wind flung hard rain against my patio door. Thunder cracked.

He smiled at me weakly. "Before we do anything," he said, "we'd best strike a bargain with Mother Nature."

He strode right out into the rain, looking up with admiration. The air was damp and cold. He smiled so broadly two deep dimples appeared in his cheeks.

"It's just beautiful," he said, turning back to me.

Big gouts of water were gushing from the downspouts and chewing up the lawn. "There goes my fucking job," I yelled over the roar. I had told him about my roofing troubles and the tenants committee with their escrow account. "I'm screwed."

He sent me for an extension ladder. When I got back, he was standing in front of Building A with four garden hoses, two over his shoulders and one in each hand. I got the ladder up against the building and fully extended. Then he gave me two of the hoses and started up. I followed.

The ladder sagged with our weight. My muddy shoes slipped against the rungs. But I followed him. When I got to the top, I was stunned to see the roof shin-deep with water. He stood there calmly flipping open his pocketknife and sawing at one of the hoses until he had an eight-foot length.

"This little barlow knife has got me out of more scrapes," he said. He knelt down, holding one end of the hose under water, then sucking on the other end, keeping his head down near the ledge. When the water started flowing, he put the end over the side and spat out a mouthful of muck.

"Tasty," he said, wiping a wet sleeve against his mouth.

I leaned out to see water sputter from the end of the hose. "Yeah!" I cried, rain whipping at my face, thunder shaking the building under my feet. I didn't care. Water was my element now. I dragged my dad to his feet, and we danced in a circle, laughing.

When we looked back, the hose had fallen over the side. It didn't matter. Quickly, we cut more lengths and set them up. I found a stack of cinder blocks by the air-conditioning unit, and we used them to anchor the hoses to the ledge. Before long, we had a dozen hoses going, a long silver rope of water spiraling from each one.

Already I could see the water level going down. When my father noticed it, he turned to me, smiling, and waded across the rooftop toward me, with his hand out for a shake. When he reached me, shining that big country-boy smile, I took his hand in mine. At first he shook it politely. Then he started pumping it hard. Then he pulled me to him and held me hard.

After we rigged up hoses on the other rooftop, we went to The Ice House, a huge bar in an old warehouse with half a dozen pool tables at one end, a dance floor in the middle, and a six-foot-wide video screen for the weekend crowd. But if you hit it right, the way we did, at about four o'clock on a weekday, it's just an acre of darkness. Nothing but quiet country blues and the sock and snick of billiard balls.

Rain rattled on the high roof, but it was a distant, comforting sound. We took a table in the middle, near the darkened dance floor. A couple sat a few tables away, dipping their heads together, whispering. A little farther away, a guy in a suit sat guarding a double bourbon. I knew the look on his face, even if I couldn't see it. In the dim light the drink was a chunk of quartz. There's no more peaceful light than the light in a good bar.

My father said he would have whatever I was having, but when the waitress brought two highballs, he only took a polite sip and put it down. I was disappointed. I wanted to get drunk with my dad.

"I don't even know what you do," I said.

"Engineer. With the navy."

"What kind of engineering?"

He looked at me steady for a few seconds, then off into the darkness. "Tomahawk, Cruise, AmRam, Boom-Boom — I've had my hand in a lot of pies."

"Sounds interesting."

"It's not what it was," he said. "It's not. The days of open-ended R and D are over. That's the truth."

He wasn't talking to me now. He was talking to some part of himself out there in the dark.

"No," he said, "this world is run by big dogs and bull-shooters." He leaned across the table and lowered his voice. "I know a man, a friend of mine, who's been working for fourteen years on a project. One day — this was just recently — they yanked him right off it. Canceled him like that." He snapped his fingers. "Told him to turn in all his reports and notes, every stitch of data he had collected over the years. But when they went to his office to get it all, they found him dancing naked around a flaming wastepaper basket. Burned up every bit of it. Guess he showed them. They pulled all his clearances and sent him for psychiatric testing. But it was worth it."

As he spoke, he played with his drink, making wet circles in the black Formica. When he finished his story, he swept up the drink and drank it straight down. The move was so quick it frightened me.

"Bug-eyed men with little tiny brains, Sparky," he said,

setting his empty glass on the table. "It's time to get out while the getting's good. I've been reading about the Cascade range, up Washington way."

"That phone call back at my place," I said. "It was the cops."

He smiled patiently. I forgive you, his smile said.

I said, "You're on the run." I didn't know what I felt about it. Ever since the phone call, I'd been seeing him as a madman one minute and a lost soul the next.

He said, "I'm on the road, if that's what you mean."

"That's not what I mean." My dad, the outlaw.

"In the heart of the Cascades, Sparky, you can live within sight of million-year-old glaciers. You can hunt and fish and never have the same meal twice. And the quiet, the peace. There's nothing like the peace of deep mountains."

When the waitress brought the next round, he raised his glass. "To J. Robert Oppenheimer," he said, "and the new physics and the Cascades and all the elk you can eat."

A woman in a cowboy shirt and jeans was dancing alone in the glow of the jukebox. She held her head low so her hair fell forward, hiding her face. Her arms were bent slightly and swung with her hips to the rhythm.

He said, "To that gal over there," and drained his glass.

"How long have you been married?" I said.

"A long time, but not for much longer." He started to snicker. "Your mother, now, there was a wonderful woman."

"You're drunk," I said.

"I'm drunk but I'm true."

I laughed, and then he laughed, and for a second we were two old friends, two drinking buddies.

By last call, we were really drunk. We wanted to get out before the lights came up and spoiled everything. The guy sitting near us was still hovering over his bourbon. As we edged past him, he looked up at me, a strand of black hair fingering his eye.

I said, "This is my dad."

He smiled a thin, bitter smile, then held up his glass. "This is my bourbon."

We walked out into a fat, slapping rain. It crashed onto car roofs. It overflowed curbs and pooled in doorways.

We drove through flooded streets to Lago Vista, rain steaming off the hood, heavy jets of water machine-gunning against the bottom of the truck. He reached under the seat and came up with a silver flask. Holding the wheel with the heels of his hands, he poured me a capful of whatever was inside.

"We need us a little nightcap," he said. He passed me the cap, then held the flask up for another toast. "Heart of the Cascades," he said, and we drank. It was applejack. After the sting, he said, "Where a man can live free of care." For the rest of the ride, he stared out the windshield, not seeing the rain, I think, seeing only trout leaping into frying pans, elk stepping into roasting pans.

He pulled the Blue Norther into the red zone next to the office, and we sat there for a little bit, just listening to the rain drum against the roof of the truck.

He squinted out at Lago Vista through the syrupy windshield. He said, "Thales, the Greek philosopher, believed the whole world was made of water." He turned to me. "Tom," he said, "you've got a fine operation here. Anyone should be right proud to live here, roof or no roof."

Rain pelted the windshield. It fell like daggers through the cold glare of the security lights. I could see that our hoses had all but stopped working, a ludicrous trickle trailing from the end of each one. The parking lot had turned into a vast wading pool.

It suddenly struck me, like a fist in the face, that my father was a madman.

"Right," I said, and held the cap out for another bellywarmer.

He studied my face as he poured. "So, what do you think?"

"About Thales?" He didn't answer.

The Cascades. My dad and me. I thought hard. A heavy gust of wind shook the truck. By morning I'd be out of a job. Soon after that, I'd have to give up my free apartment. And then it would be debt collectors day and night.

I popped the door and stepped out into the shattering rain. It felt like cold electricity. I turned to face him. The Cascades.

He said, "The whole world made of water." He shook his head. "That fellow had to be a sailor."

Sometimes, when I was a kid, my father would come out in the street with me after supper. We'd throw my football around. He taught me where to place my fingers, how to put some spin on the ball. He taught me how to run and catch, and how to keep the ball safe in the cradle of my arm. After a few light tosses, he'd start to back off.

"Go long," he'd say, and I'd run down the darkening street, happy as a dog. I watched him over my shoulder as I ran, the way he cocked his arm, the way he sent the ball soaring as high as the treetops. He had a good arm.

We'd stay out way after dark, and the passes would get longer and longer, the ball thrown from a great distance, thrown blind.

"Go long," he says, and I run, half the block, three-quarters of the block, so far away I can't even see him throw. But I see the ball flash up near the streetlight, then lose itself in the dark again. And always, when I think it won't ever come down, the ball breaks into sight, spinning smoothly into my hands.

I thought those nights would last forever, when I ran in the dark street, breathless, believing in my father's arm.

The Small Things
That Save Us

THE FIRST TIME I SAW EASY, HE WAS STANDING in the
middle of the road, a one-armed man kicking the big back
tire of a tractor, slapping at it with his hat. It was a small
tractor, an old gray Ford held together with baling wire and
electrical tape. After we rolled it onto the shoulder, I drove
him back to his farm.

He had about forty head of cattle on twenty-five acres
that sloped into a shallow valley. The top ten acres were
fenced off and full of timothy, tall and shimmering in the
wind. The rest was pasture and woodland. He didn't seem
worried about the tractor. But then, it wouldn't start for some
thief any easier than it had done for him.

I stayed for supper, though at first Joan, his wife, seemed
nervous at having a stranger in her house. Their boy must
have been the quietest four-year-old on record. Jimmy. We
had chicken, mashed potatoes, and peas, but he would only
eat slices of buttered bread.

Easy was the kind of man who likes to run the talk at supper.

"Those cows of mine are stupid on purpose," he said. From the kitchen window, we could see them coming up the lane and crowding together in the holding pen, moaning at the closed barn door. Big dull eyes, and smaller than any cows I had ever seen. They were full-grown yet stood only waist-high.

"All the smarts got bred out so they'd be easy to handle. And being small, they need less acreage. They're the latest thing."

Easy was Frank Nagle. He had brown shaggy hair that looked like he cut it himself, in the dark. He and Joan were thirty, thirty-five. She was taller than Easy by a couple inches. She wore faded jeans and one of his flannel shirts that had seen too much work and washing. The colors were faded and the cloth was limp and threadbare, but that only brought out her beauty. She had a generous look that told you the things you said mattered to her.

Easy rubbed the stub of his right arm. "It was one of those things you warn everybody else about, then all of a sudden you just can't believe it's happening to you."

I could see Joan tense up as she listened to a story she must have heard many times.

"Corn got caught in my picker," he said, "so I went back to unclog it. Forgot to turn the damn thing off. It grabbed my hand, pulled the whole arm in.

"Caddy Leboux, my neighbor, he came running when he heard the screams. He says he found me jammed up against the picker, with my arm being clawed to pieces inside. I was unconscious by then. He says the damn picker wouldn't let me fall. He had to take the son-of-a-bitch apart to get me loose. I got my name because I can do things easier with one arm than most can with two."

"Except when it comes to cleaning up after himself," Joan said.

After supper he and I sat on the back porch and drank like hillbillies, from a big brown crock. Once a month he visited a cousin in West Virginia. He called it his "moon run." Moonshine.

We left the porch light off to keep the bugs away. Barn swallows had built a nest in the space above the fixture. We'd watch them come dipping up the long slope toward the house and then swoop above us to the nest. All evening it was like that, sitting in the dark, drinking Easy's moon.

He wanted to take out a loan so he could fence in more pasture and buy more "mini-cows." Hard work for a one-armed man. Maybe it was that, or the drinking, or just the good feeling I had sitting there, but I offered to stay and help out.

He looked at me a little suspiciously and took a pull from the crock. "If it's money you're after, there isn't any."

"I'm only after food and a place to stay," I said.

He was quiet for a while. Then he said, "Let's sleep on this. See if it sounds good sober."

Next morning he showed me a whitewashed shack about a hundred yards below the house, two rooms attached to a potting shed.

"My idea was to have a place to hide when the Russians drop the bomb. But then Caddy Leboux told me about radiation, so that was that. Now I come down here when Joan kicks me out. I poison my liver and argue with the empty rooms. You fix it up any way you like."

The front room had a moldy cot, a potbellied stove, and a pile of firewood. In the kitchen were a Formica table and two rusty chairs with split, sun-bleached seat pads. The electric stove didn't work, and the sink had no drainpipe, just an open hole to the floor. Canned food was stacked on wooden shelves all around the room — ham, peaches, tomatoes, peas — a whole truckload. I got used to heating cans on the wood stove.

The shack was a wreck, but one wall of the front room had a homemade picture window that looked out over the farm. The light in those fields was pure luxury. Country light. Clean. I'd sit and stare for hours, listening to birds circling through the trees, to wind hissing in the long grass.

Easy and I got on well together, with me doing the heavy work and him dealing with feed suppliers and the bank. His farm was not a moneymaker, but he was serious, he had plans. And little by little, we thought, we could turn the place around. Those huge farms you see, they're all science. A small farm like Easy's is a record of the farmer's life. Sometimes it's a record of the failures and mistakes and accidents that make a life. So it was important for us to do things right. The farm was a kind of fresh start for Easy. He had bought it a few years back, when he and Joan married, using inheritance money he hadn't already drunk or gambled away. He liked to say that Joan's love saved his life. It embarrassed me whenever he said that, the sentimentality of it.

The first snow came in early October, right when money was getting scarce. One evening Easy and Joan started yelling at each other and slamming doors. I could hear some of it all the way to the shack, maybe because of the way sound carries over snowy ground. Maybe because misery carries over any ground.

She said, ". . . cows . . . loser . . . farm . . . lunatic."

Then Easy, louder: ". . . beat me . . . I'll be damned . . ." I heard glass breaking. The TV came on loud. Some goofy cartoon voice sang, "Take good care of yourself, like your friend Shamu!" Then the TV went off, and I didn't hear anything for a long time.

A little later I went up near the house to burn some trash. All through the fight, Jimmy was out there playing in the snow, rolling snowballs that kept falling apart. He looked like a small blue astronaut in his snow gear. He was talking and singing to himself, words I couldn't make out. The barrel of trash was in full blaze. I poked at it with a broom handle so it crackled and roared. Sparks shot up in bright showers and fell on the snow. It was late. It had been quiet for a long time.

When I looked up, Easy and Joan were standing on the back porch. They clung to each other like they had just staggered out of a burning house, like it was all they could do to stand up. She was crying a little with her head against his shirt, stroking his chest. There were tears in his eyes, too. They stood there on the porch in the cold, staring off down the hill. He held her close and kissed her hair without taking his eyes off the darkness. They were holding each other so tight it was like they were afraid they might fly apart.

Easy called to the boy, his voice raw and weak. The boy walked toward them and climbed the back steps slowly.

When you're four years old, I think, the world goes on pretty much without you. You find the safe places where you can. He climbed those stairs like an old man coming home from a long day of field work. His house was safe again, for a little while at least. The three of them went inside. Lights came on upstairs and, after a time, went out again. There was nothing left but the night and the snow and flames spraying into the cold wind.

One warm day late in October, I started digging postholes. It was the wrong season for that sort of work, but we were anxious to get the field ready for the new cows. Digging postholes was something a one-armed man couldn't do. He was off at the Agway and the bank. After a few holes, I went up to the house for a beer. Joan was standing at the sink, her hands in soapy water, just staring out at the farm.

Her windowsill was full of cuttings in jelly jars. Coleus. Wandering Jew. Swedish ivy. We got to talking, like neighbors over a back fence. I don't know what brought us together that day. Unless it was the cuttings, like a sign of hope, the late-afternoon light sloping through the windows, her hair shining in that pale gold light: we make up stories to carry ourselves through the longest nights, and this is mine.

She took my hand and led me upstairs, where we made love like old friends who thought they'd never see each other again. Slow and solemn love. Later we talked. Easy was her second husband. Frank, she called him.

"I was married first to Big John, Jimmy's father. He was a small, spiteful man with corns on his vocal cords from screaming at wrestlers on the TV."

I was lying on my back, listening to Joan, listening for the sound of Easy's pickup. Already the feelings that had made it all seem so natural were starting to fade. I think she knew that, and that's why she kept talking.

"Big John worked in a heat-treating plant. Anchor chains, gun barrels, cam shafts, and the like. Dangerous work. The furnaces would heat up to eighteen hundred degrees. Sometimes an oil bath would burst into flame and blow out every window in the place. Two men died there, and Big John was one of them. He fell off an I-beam into a vat of caustic soda. When I'm feeling truly mean about the past, I like to say all they could fish out was his rodeo belt buckle. But the truth is he survived, at least for a while. He swallowed some of that slop, though, and died later from pneumonia."

She rolled so she was leaning on her elbow, looking down at me, her loose hair shading her face. She said, "The day I married Frank, my heart was in my mouth. Without him, I would just turn into some kind of character."

Joan was sweet and strong, and I loved her in a way that

afternoon, but when Easy's pickup pulled in, I was back in the field, chopping at the cold ground, feeling cheap and lonely.

I don't know a thing about cattle. Before the snow I'd sit in the shack and watch them graze. Cowbirds sat on their shoulders. Flies swarmed in their eyes. Nothing bothered those cows. Easy was right about how stupid they were. When I ran a water line to the field and attached a noser, it took them all day to learn how to nuzzle the paddle for fresh water.

They'd walk the fence, looking for a break into the wild grapes on the other side. During storms they'd huddle under the lean-to. It was nothing but sapling trunks and sheets of tin, but it was sturdy. Then they found out they could scratch an itch by rubbing against the roof supports. Each day that roof was more and more crooked. Someday, I figured, it would come right down on them.

When Easy couldn't get his price for the cows, he decided to keep them through winter. Lots of farmers did that — kept cattle, siloed grain — waiting for a better market. But there was the extra cost. We had a barn full of hay, a little corn. Feed, though, all that extra Super Fit-n-Fresh — that was expensive. Easy couldn't get his price because the buyers said there wasn't enough meat on the new breed. They said the cows were all bone. But Easy didn't see it that way. He would keep those cows, he said, until he found a buyer who wasn't out to cheat him.

Things began to fall apart when the feed started running low. At night I'd hear the cows groaning and butting the barn door. They wanted to graze, I guess, but they couldn't, not with two feet of snow on the ground and more falling all the time.

Pretty soon the grain was gone. I pitched plenty of hay to them, but they needed more than that to keep up their body heat. They kicked at the pens when they saw the hay dropping down. Big whucking kicks that splintered wood. Later, as they passed the silo on their way to the field, they licked the feeding auger, but when they saw it was no use, they stamped the ground, tails switching like whips.

One evening a couple weeks later I noticed some of them hadn't come back to the barn. Three of them were lying against one another in the lean-to. They didn't seem to have the strength to make it up the hill. That night the temperature dropped to twenty below. By morning they were dead.

For days I couldn't look at them. I hoped the drifting snow would cover them up, but no. The other cows wouldn't go near the lean-to. More died, in the field, in the lane that went down to the field, in the barn. Easy'd gone to all the feed suppliers in the valley, but his credit was stretched to the limit and the bank wouldn't give him a break. He just sat on the porch all day in the cold, drinking his cousin's home brew and staring at the cows as if they had betrayed him.

It was one of those days when the sun is so bright and the cold so cutting that you can hardly stand it. I had just stepped out of the shack and was waiting for my eyes to adjust to the glare. Jimmy was out there, beside a red plastic sled loaded with kindling, a piece of rope, a few handfuls of snow, other trash. He stared up at me.

"He says to give you this."

The note said, "Let's fall by The Farmer's and do some damage."

Jimmy was almost crying, his voice like a prayer: "You're hurting my shadow."

I stepped away from him. His small shadow lay sprawled on the snow, its chest caved in by my footprints.

When I got to the house, Easy was coming out the door.

Joan followed, saying, "You were my hope against hope. Do you hear? I thought ... but look at us, Frank. Look at us."

Jimmy had followed me up the hill. Now he emptied the heavy sled onto the snow, singing quietly to himself.

Easy threw things into the back of his pickup — rope, stray lumber, a sack of rock salt. I think he wanted to hear what she had to say but didn't want her to know it.

He said, "Don't lay it all on me, Joan." He said her name as if it were a dirty word. He stomped around the truck, kicking it, banging his fist against it. We climbed into the cab and he yelled, "I'm bitched! I'm bitched!"

Joan was at my window. I rolled it down. "Talk to him," she said. "Knock some sense into the pigheaded cripple." She pushed off the truck and went back to the house. Easy pumped the gas hard and swung into the road.

When we were away from the house, he looked at me and

broke out laughing. "Pigheaded cripple! God, I love that woman!"

At The Farmer's Inn we drank a few beers and threw some darts. Easy's shots kept hitting the wall.

He said, "It's a rag arm, but it's the only arm I got. Let's say you won. Anyway, the soup here's a killer, and I'm hungry."

A few farmers were sitting around with their caps pushed back on their heads, sipping beers and rubbing their chins. They nodded at Easy as if they knew his trouble but weren't going to be the ones to bring it up.

"Sure, my head's hard," Easy said to me as we sat down at a table. "I'm a pigheaded cripple! After this is all over, I'm going to have to get me a new nickname. Pig. That'd be it, I guess."

He unpinned his sleeve and reached up inside to scratch his stub. "You know what I miss?" he said, looking down at his empty sleeve, his voice softening. "I had the prettiest little dragon tattoo. Right about here." He touched the sleeve where his forearm had been. "Isn't that the damnedest thing? I miss my tattoo."

The old woman behind the bar brought us two bowls of split pea. "Soup's good today," she said.

"Soup's good every day," Easy said. "I like this place. Never saw a single unruly drunk here. Gerry, here, is really something. She saved me many times in the bad old days. Helped me face up to my weaselly ways."

Gerry said, "Thank you, kind sir," and kissed his forehead, like a blessing.

As I ate my soup, I thought about Joan and that afternoon months before. "You don't know me very well, Easy," I said.

"I know your work," he said. "You learn a thing about a man when you see him work. That's enough for me."

"I could be some kind of escapee," I said.

"I thought of that, at first, when you wanted to stay on. But then I thought, what've we got to steal?"

I laughed and he said, "You married? I know it's none of my business, but you have a look. You married?"

"Not in the eyes of the law," I said.

"Not in the eyes of the law. Now, that's sad as can be. When you came to the farm, I figured you were broke down. Joan said your car looked fine to her, and I said no, it was more than that. That's all we needed to know. She trusts you the same as me."

"You shouldn't trust me," I said. "Easy," I said, "people do things. They don't mean to, but they do them. Later they're sorry, but the harm is already done."

"You planning on robbing us after all?" he said, scraping at the green sludge on the bottom of his bowl.

"You're not listening to me. I've done something I'm ashamed of, and I have to tell you."

Easy looked up then and sipped his beer, his eyes going over me.

"A little while ago," I said, "I was working in the field. I went to the house for a beer. Joan and I got to talking."

"That woman is a great one for talking. Sometimes she's quiet for days. And then it's like a dam burst — everything just rushes right out."

"Easy," I said, and for the first time it seemed like a foolish name to say.

"She takes her time thinking about a thing. She'll talk about it only after she has it figured out in her mind. She's deeper than me, and I admire that."

"Easy, something happened between Joan and me that afternoon."

"I know," he said quietly. "You spent time together." He was looking down at the rings of wetness his bottle had made on the tablecloth. He ran his hand through his shaggy hair. He looked tired.

"I'm sorry, Frank."

"Only Joan calls me Frank," he said. "Nobody else."

I said, "I wish it never happened. I wish we didn't have this standing between us."

"When Joan told me, first I was mad. Then I cried. I thought she was leaving me. But she said it was just something that happened, naturally, between friends. She doesn't lie to me. I know enough to listen to her. I'm not that pigheaded. I used to be a drunk and a runaround. I know that life — do the worst and don't get caught. Joan settled me down. She opened my eyes. If you're sorry because you hurt me, well, that's one thing. To that I say, I'll live. But if you're sorry it happened, that's something else. I don't really think you are. Do you?"

I don't know how to account for the calm in some people. Easy was a one-armed man watching his life fall apart. I was the stranger who stole his wife one afternoon. But we spent hours in The Farmer's, talking and laughing about bills that were past due, money beyond our reach, and the line of useless postholes I had dug.

By the time we got home, the evening was setting in. We stood awkwardly near the steps of the side door. He gripped my shoulder. There was a lot of strength in that hand. Then he moved his rough palm up against the side of my neck and held it there. He looked at me the way a woman looks at you in the dark when the stars are right, making you forget what you're afraid of.

I said, "Easy, this afternoon, before we left, I heard Jimmy out here. You know how he sings all the time? Well, I finally heard what he's singing: 'Cows are brown, cows are gray, cows are in the field all day.' "

He shook his head at the dead cattle lying in the field. "That's not fair to him. He shouldn't have to see that. What have I been thinking?"

Earlier that day, as Easy and Joan argued, Jimmy had stood quietly chanting his song. His wagonload of junk was the most important thing in his life at that moment — an empty cigarette pack, a saucer, a cracked clay pot, an old medicine jar.

"We got unfinished business."

After hooking up the backhoe, I drove the tractor down the icy, rutted lane running along the far edge of the farm. Easy rode behind, with one foot on the axle and the other on the backhoe, so I drove slow. The tractor almost shook itself apart as it lurched and slid over the hard ground. Twice the engine died, and in the silence I could feel the presence of the dead cattle lying in the field beside us. The clouds were faint scraps of shadow far away, and the stars were beginning to show.

They lay in the dark field like mounds of freshly turned earth. Heavy black birds strutted back and forth over the bloated carcasses, their broad, oily wings snapping viciously.

Halfway down the lane I yelled to Easy over the engine's roar. "Let's dig it in the woods, OK?"

He nodded a few times, but I'm not sure he heard me. I wanted the grave to be hidden, so I drove to a clearing deep in the woods. It was darker there and felt colder, despite the windbreak of pine, cedar, and laurel. Easy walked off into the trees. He must have figured he wouldn't be much help, and that probably embarrassed him.

I set to work on the grave, but every time I brought the backhoe against the icy ground, the tractor's engine strained and choked and nearly died. I gave it a little more gas and shifted into the lowest gear. Nothing worked.

Finally, cold and angry, I yanked the prong of the throttle toward me, ripping it over the metal notches on its scale. The engine roared with the rich gasoline, the backhoe bit into the ground, but then sour black smoke began to pour from the engine, the roar became an aching metal shriek, and the whole thing shuddered into silence.

I jumped down, cursing myself and the tractor. My feet were cold, my breath came in plumes. The stars glowed weakly over the bristle of trees at the edge of the clearing.

Easy called to me from deeper in the woods. I thought he was yelling at me for burning out the engine, but he wanted me to bring the wire cutters.

I climbed over some fallen trees and stepped across a narrow, frozen stream. I couldn't move quickly, because of the rocks and roots hidden beneath the snow.

He was standing near the border fence, rubbing the back of his neck and moaning a little. One of the cows had become caught in the barbed wire that ran between Easy's place and Leboux's.

He said, "At first I thought it might be a boulder, the woods are so dark. Then I saw it clear. Then I knew."

The cow had tried to push its head between the top two strings and step through, but it had fouled itself and fallen into the wire. The posts on either side strained and creaked with its weight.

He said, "I feel so awful. This is all my fault."

"It was an accident, Easy. It just happened, that's all."

The cow had not died right away. It must have struggled against the sharp wire with the last of its strength. Blood stood as thick as jelly in the long, twisting grooves the wire had cut into its flesh. The carcass was pitched forward, with its head hanging just a few inches above the dark, crusty snow. A frozen yellow beard of drool hung from its mouth.

One string of wire had caught the long jaw, holding it like a strap. One hind leg was strung up so it barely touched the ground. The other was splayed and twisted in midair by the wire. Both forelegs were bent and bound against the stomach.

"We got to cut it free," Easy said.

"It's dead. What good will that do?"

He turned to me. His face was rashy and swollen from the cold. "We can't leave it like this," he said.

I set the metal jaw of the snip against the wire, near the cow's head, and bit into it. The wire sprang into spiky coils as the carcass fell forward onto the ground.

The cow was still alive. It gave a long screaming moan of pain and then struggled to stand. One hind leg was still hung up in the wire. The other kept slipping on the snow. Its eyes were wide and white. I could see its fat black tongue behind its bared teeth. Then it swung its bloody head into my chest.

Easy said, "Oh my God, my God . . . ."

The cow screamed again, a rising groan of terror. It tried to shake its hind leg free but couldn't. Just then its forelegs buckled and the cow crashed down for the last time, one eye rolling in its socket, then trembling, then congealing to ice. The cow lay there on the bloody snow, finally dead.

There was nothing we could do. We left the tractor and the cow, and made our way back through the woods toward home. When we got to the stone wall at the edge of the field, we sat down. Easy kneaded his stump and stared.

He said, "What was I thinking when I bought those cows? They're none of them any good."

My lungs burned and my ribs ached from where the cow had hit me. I said, "That tractor's a piece of junk, too."

"That tractor's a forty-nine Ford. It's a classic," he said. "You just got it all gummed up."

"I think I ruined it," I said.

"No, no. We'll just give it a good swift kick in the morning. That's the thing about a classic."

"I hope you're right," I said. "I hope we can get them buried."

The shadows of clouds crossing the moon floated over the field.

"This is a terrible thing," Easy said. "I sure messed things up good. Some farmer I am. Some kind of farmer."

"Look," I said. "You can see the house from here." I pointed a quarter mile uphill at the porch light glowing weakly. It was like the sudden light you find sometimes in deep woods. All you expect is darkness and shadow. Then a shaft of moonlight spills onto the ground just where you set your foot. It's a small thing, but it makes you think you should keep walking.

Overhead, the night hardened around its cold stars. Maybe there were things he could have done. He could have sold off some acreage or unloaded the cattle at any price. But there really wasn't time. And anyway, that didn't matter. The only thing that mattered was the way he and Joan stood on the back porch that night, clinging to each other, while out there in the dark their dreams were dying.

What happens happens. The day rises and the night falls. Troubles turn on you before you bat an eye. "Should have" and "could have" don't count. Your house is in flames and the world is made of ice.

Easy stood and said, "I'm never going to be the same."

But he was wrong. He would be all right. Easy would let the small things save him. Days of sun and sweet breezes. Late afternoons full of birds streaming into trees. And other shadows on other nights, as deer climb down from the high ground to the stream in moonlight.

Encantado

W HEN I WAS YOUNG I THOUGHT THE CITY would save
me. New York. Manhattan. Island of light. I thought it would
rescue me from the dead-end days and nights of the Pennsylvania factory town where I grew up. Later I got to know a
woman who felt the same way. Cary. Right after graduation
we got married and moved here. Well, to Brooklyn.

All day I enter data for Pharma-Tech, a drug information
service. We keep computer records of disease and drug inter-
actions, metabolic dysfunctions, chemical tolerances, tox-
icity, spectrums of activity. It's just a glorified typing job, but it
gives me the chills. Malacoplakia, arthralgia, erythropoietic
protoporphyria . . . all the diseases we enter hour after hour.
I can't stop thinking about them, can't stop wondering which
strange seed has sprouted inside Cary.

She's a small woman, who shops in the junior miss department and wears her long brown hair in pigtails because she
just feels like it. She has always been a little out of touch. She
loses money, forgets where she's left things. Sometimes she's

gone for hours because she can't remember the way home and she's too embarrassed to call. I've never bothered her about these things. I like to think a happy marriage means staying out of each other's way.

This morning, as I walk into the data lab, another word processor invites me to dinner. Mercer's face is pale, freckled. He keeps his hair clipped short. He has the taut features of an anorexic. He's so thin he's narrow, a slice of human being.

"Alejandro — he's my lover — his mom's here from Mexico. She wants to cook for him, clean, do the mother thing." We grab stacks of pharmacy reports and head for our terminals. He keeps talking as he inputs data from the first report. It's that kind of job. "The truth, Mikey, is that she wants to check out Handy's dirty-minded friends." He turns to me, his wide, wet mouth twisted with disappointment. He strokes one index finger across the top of the other. The shame-shame sign. I haven't seen it since I was a kid. "I want her to think Handy knows some straight guys. So come, OK?"

When Mercer and Handy pick me up at eight, it's already getting dark. I'm waiting for them on the front steps of my building. Cary's been in the hospital for two weeks, and I've kind of given up on cleaning.

As they climb out of Mercer's Accord, they seem to be arguing. But then I see they're only fooling around. They come up on each side of me like I need to be guided to the curb. Handy's face is broad and brown. His skin shines. He's wearing loose white pants and a shirt with flowing sleeves to hide his extra weight.

"How bad can it be?" Mercer says. He's wearing gray chinos and a navy blue polo shirt.

"You have no idea!" Handy says. And then, to me, "He has no idea! My mother's been here three days and I'm worn out, I'm fed up." When he talks, his hands talk. They flash like birds. "I can't get her out of the apartment! I say, 'Mama, let's go up the Empire State Building.' No. I say, 'Don't you want to see Lady Liberty?' No. I bring her programs and brochures from Radio City, the Metropolitan, the Museum of Natural History. But she won't leave the apartment. She points at her head and says, 'Everything I need to see, I see in here.'"

The street smells like damp laundry from the on-and-off rain we've had all day. As I climb into the backseat of the car, Handy says, "And people, people, people. All the time they're in the apartment, lined up in the hall. First it was only the people in my building. Now they come from all over the city. They want her magic. That old buffalo's going to get me evicted!" Mercer pulls into traffic as Handy rolls down his window and yells, "My mother is crazy!" He's so excited his voice goes up and his accent gets thicker. "Craycee!"

Mercer says, "I don't know why you want to turn the little mother into a tourist. As far as natural history goes, I can tell her all she needs to know about her little *niño*."

Handy punches him lightly in the shoulder several times. Mercer yelps and lets go of the wheel to protect himself. The car drifts toward the double line. Handy grabs the wheel. Mercer steps a little harder on the gas.

"Here," he says, reaching into his shirt pocket. "It's happy hour. One for you and you and me." He presses something into Handy's mouth, then reaches back over the seat and drops one into my hand. A tiny blood-red pill stamped in the shape of a heart. Mercer swallows his and finally takes the wheel again.

"What is it?" I ask, poking it around on my palm.

"Love speed," Handy says dreamily. He's leaning back against the headrest now, waiting for the drug to kick in. "I gave them to Mercer last Valentine's Day. These are the last ones, so enjoy." Without looking, he reaches for Mercer's right hand, pulls it away from the wheel, and laces fingers.

In the mirror, Mercer sees me staring at the pill. "Come on," he says, "exuberate yourself."

"Maybe later," I say, dropping the pill into my shirt pocket. I'm thinking of Cary, of nurses with pills in paper cups. We pass a Chinese restaurant, its window strung with slaughtered poultry.

Things are quiet for a while, nothing but the sound of traffic whizzing through the gray streets, and Handy's murmuring. He's tugging on Mercer's hand. He says, *"Mi compadre."* He says, *"Mi pollo."*

The third time we pass the Chinese restaurant, I say, "Mercer, we're driving in circles."

With wonder in his voice, as if we've been allowed to witness a miracle, he says, "I know. Rectangles, actually, we're doing rectangles." They laugh, too long, too loud. Then Handy reaches for the sunroof control, and Mercer slaps his hand away. He reaches for it again, and Mercer slaps his hand away. It goes on like that until Handy says, "Mercer *ees* so *seely!*"

Mercer shoots back, "Don't play dumb wetback with me, Paco!"

Cary and I used to have fun. Someone gave us a small ceramic dinosaur filled with maraschino liqueur. Bomba — that's what she called it — began to turn up at the breakfast table, its heavy lip nudging the edge of her plate.

"Bomba is hungry," she'd say, holding a corner of toast to its mouth. "Bomba wants a Denver omelet."

At first it was funny. But one night the turquoise dinosaur was standing on her pillow. "Bomba doesn't like me," she said, backing away from the bed. "Bomba doesn't like me." I buried it deep in the kitchen garbage, but in the morning it was standing next to the orange juice, its head and plated back pebbly with coffee grounds. "Bomba doesn't like me." On the way to work, I gave it to someone on the subway.

That night at dinner she shook out her napkin, leaned over, and tied her ankle to the leg of her chair. She saw me staring and said, "So I won't float away." I smiled at her, but she just looked at me.

When I woke up the next morning, she had torn a sheet into strips, knotted them together, and leashed herself to the bed frame. It was long enough to take her to the bathroom, the couch, the stove, no longer. During the day, she'd hold it gathered in her arms like the train of a gown, playing it out as she moved around the apartment and, when it got caught, gently whipping it free of the furniture. At night she'd sleep under an open dictionary. Even then I didn't say anything, do anything.

A few days later the apartment felt strangely empty when I came home. I called her name. Then I followed the soft rope of her leash across the floor to the hall closet. She was crouching naked inside, trembling, her fingers jammed into her mouth. I don't know what happened to her. I don't know. It was like something in her came undone.

At the hospital they made me feel like a criminal waiting to be charged. They were right. I was guilty of not trying to save her.

Outside, the city funnels past Mercer's car. I'm perched between the seats, between Mercer's close-cropped head and Handy's, the long black hair caught up in a little ponytail. His "rat tail," Mercer calls it. I feel like a kid in the back seat of his parents' car. It's dark back here. There are too many things I don't know how to say.

Then we're on the bridge, tires whining against metal. Handy says, "I am sick to the death of my mother."

Mercer says, "I know what let's do. Let's have a quick one at Harlow's."

I say, "What about dinner? What about Handy's mother?"

"What about her?" Handy says. "She's *my* mother."

"Look," Mercer says, fake tough. "If you're going to freak, we'll throw you right through the window."

Handy curls up in his seat and kicks the dashboard, laughing.

Harlow's is on Fifty-second, a long way from Handy's place on the Lower East Side. It's full of gleaming chrome, gray plush, black-and-white stills of Jean Harlow. HARLOW'S is written out in blue neon along the wall behind the bar. On another wall, a large screen is playing MTV. The band members are throwing their hair around, the camera is swirling, but somebody has turned off the sound and put on Sinatra. "Angel Eyes."

The place is full of men who look like corporate lawyers and yachtsmen. On our way to the bar, we pass someone Mercer knows, a tall man in a gray suit cut to show off his narrow waist. He has spent more on his hair than I've spent on my whole wardrobe, including shoes. His face is deeply, unnaturally, expensively tanned.

"Stephen," Mercer says, taking one of the man's hands in both of his. "This is my lover, Handy. And this . . . this is, well, Mikey." Stephen's smile is easy. His face creases in interesting ways. He holds my hand too long, covers it lightly, for a moment, with the other. I smile at the cliché of it. Mercer jerks away from us and walks stiffly to the bar.

He has already ordered a round of kamikazes by the time Handy and I get there. He pushes a couple of barstools aside and says, "The only dignified way to drink at a bar is to stand. Besides, it shows off the clothes. Did you see how wrinkled he was?" Handy doesn't say anything. He's leaning back against the bar, staring after Stephen. In the wash of blue light from the neon sign, Mercer looks extraterrestrial.

I say, "You called Handy your 'lover.' Doesn't that embarrass you? I mean, it does me. I wouldn't introduce a woman to anyone as my 'lover.' Even the thought of it . . ." I look away. I never talked to them about Cary before she went into the hospital, so I can't exactly start now.

"You wouldn't because you couldn't," Mercer says, his mouth going wide. "To love you, a woman would have to be stone blind and *dee*ranged." I wait for him to laugh, but he keeps at me, his eyes dead level with mine, his voice calm. "You're the dog nobody wants, Mikey. You're here out of pity. I

179

thought you knew that." He stares at me with his flat eyes, as if to tell me this is no joke, or this is the biggest joke. I take a long, slow sip of my drink.

Two weeks ago at this time I was handing my wife a bouquet of limp violets in the locked ward. An orderly sat with us. He wasn't necessary. She and I were both sedated in our ways. I was carrying a pint in my coat pocket. We talked for twenty minutes. About what? I can't remember.

I brought her blue flannel nightgown from home because the hospital gown gave her a rash. I remember thinking the nightgown was so old, so washed out, that no one but me knew what color it really was. I wanted to tell someone.

Before I left, Cary leaned close to me — in simple tenderness, I thought, or to make a promise, or to confess my crime. "I think," she said — she put her hand on mine — "I think all those who die suddenly, like in a bus accident, are very sad and will be resurrected, all those who believe in Jesus Christ, and in the night in my room there are spirits who try to hurt me and hurt my womb." She climbed into her hospital bed and strapped one wrist into a Velcro restraint. She smiled sadly and held the other wrist out, helpless. I laid it in the cuff and pulled the strap across.

At the door, I turned to say goodbye again. I saw the faded blue nightgown, the hard white sheets, the Velcro straps, the cracked window a few feet from her bed. I told myself you can't save anyone. I told myself you shouldn't even try. I haven't had the courage to see her since.

Across the barroom, Stephen has stopped to talk to three

men who look like extras from the cast of *Melrose Place.*
Handy gives out a low whistle. "That Stephen," he says.

I say, "He seems very pleasant, doesn't he?" and I know
exactly what I'm doing. Mercer's got an ugly look on his face,
like he wants to bite off the edge of his glass. In the blue neon
his freckles look black.

"That man," Handy says, still gazing at Stephen, "is a
walking smorgasbord."

When Mercer speaks I can see teeth marks on his lower
lip. He says, quietly, intensely, "That man is probably full of
viruses, fungi, parasites, and mycobacteria, but you go ahead,
Paco. Partake. And when you get sick — because you *will* get
sick — I'll nurse you. And when your numbers start drifting
down, when you're jumping from one antiviral to another, I'll
be there. Through the fevers, the night sweats, and the pain
that rips up your insides. Don't be afraid. You won't die alone.
I'll nurse you right through to the end, Paco. I'll sing you to
sleep with the names of your diseases." And he begins to
chant: "Fungal meningitis, Kaposi's sarcoma, lymphoma,
Pneumocystis carinii, T-cell deficiency. . . ."

Handy, I think, has stopped breathing. I'm scared for him.
I want to hurt Mercer.

"Still," I say, tipping some ice into my mouth, "you have to
admit, that fellow's a real looker." Before Mercer can come back
at me, I say, "You know what we need? More liquor!" I catch the
bartender. "You see this freckle-faced boy?" I'm shaking Mercer
by the shoulders. "This boy didn't have a mother. I know so from
him." I hook my thumb at Handy, but he's just leaning over his

empty glass. I slap Mercer on the back a little harder than I mean to. "This boy here was suckled by a wild pig."

Mercer blinks a few times, like he's coming out of a trance. He finds his drink and says, "I'll thank you not to malign the mum," downing the last of it. Then he steps closer to Handy and lightly touches the back of his neck. A look passes between them. I swear I can feel the touch on my own skin.

"Nurse," I say to the bartender, "we'll have three more of your kazzamazzis."

The bartender bends down to the liquor rail, then straightens up, grins. "My kazza whatzkis?"

Mercer steps back from me and stares. Handy gives me a sidelong grin and flips his drink straw at me.

"Three more . . . zakamazzis," I say, playing along, getting back on top. "Three more . . . Edmund Muskies." Handy slaps the bar top. Mercer gives me this am-I-mortified look. "Bartender?" I try again. "A trio of your finest . . . sudsy huskies."

Handy calls out, "That's right, sweets! Bring on them husky Russkis!" He's laughing, and now Mercer's laughing. They're laughing so hard I think things might turn out all right.

The drive down the East Side takes a long time, but it's pleasant. Manhattan is lit up. Even the ships on the waterfront are strung with lights. Wind stiffens the river, turning the black water back on itself. A searchlight fans at the night sky. Our tires hiss through the thin wetness laid down by a shower that fell while we were in the bar. It's late summer, impossible to predict the weather.

Mercer finally pulls the car to a stop at the edge of a run-down neighborhood. Here and there, newly renovated tenements stand out, their brickwork sandblasted clean. Handy lives in one of them. "Just a few blocks from here," he says. "A few blocks," Mercer says, his head bobbing. "Right."

We pass boarded-up shops, mountains of garbage piled high against parked cars. It feels late. We're tired, coming down a little. The dinner has turned into an awful duty.

As if he's read my mind, Handy whimpers, "Mama, I don't want to come in yet. I want to stay out with my friends!"

"Sweetpea," Mercer says softly, "you don't have any friends."

But Handy's moving out ahead of us now, doing dance steps as he walks, swinging his hips, watching the way his legs twist. He's up on point now. He's whirling around, his big sleeves billowing out. He shouts, "I'm Rita Moreno!"

Mercer says, "You're a calypso nightmare."

"You're the Swamp Thing," I toss out lamely. Every word makes them laugh. I see now that it's the fact that they're laughing that makes them laugh. They cackle and howl. I feel like I've come to the party late and everyone's already drunk.

The street is filled with men on motorcycles. Three of them, their leather jackets blistered with studs and buckles, are passing a bottle. One looks like a huge leather balloon. The air shudders, blue with exhaust, engines boiling and popping.

"This is my block," Handy says.

Mercer stops us before we pass the bikers and says, "Walk tough."

I say, "What?"

"Walk tough. We didn't want to tell you before. We didn't want you to freak. This is where the Angels hang."

"What angels?"

"*The* Angels. East Coast. Chapter 666." Mercer and Handy start walking in a half-slouch, a slow-motion swagger. But when they see themselves they lose it and fall against each other. Handy leans back, cups his hands around his mouth, and calls out, "Lucy! I'm home!"

I'm trying to be calm, but red vultures are spray-painted everywhere, there are bullet holes in the bricked-over storefronts. Are my arms swinging too much as I walk? Not enough? But the bikers pay no attention. When we go by, the leather balloon passes the bottle and says, "To my way of thinking, when in doubt, knock them out."

Handy looks at me seriously and whispers, "Mercer was scared, too, when he first came here. Don't worry. Nobody gets killed on this block unless the Angels do the killing. And the Angels don't do no killing unless you bother them."

"Like bees," I say. Mercer and Handy break into another fit of laughter.

"Look," Handy says, "I'm telling you it's the safest neighborhood in New York." One of the bikers flings an empty bottle against a tenement wall. Handy makes a face. "Really!"

We're climbing the stairs. The air is heavy with heat and strange smells, something sharp that makes my nostrils flare, something muggy and dull. A stereo is playing somewhere. I don't hear the music so much as feel it, the bass pounding in my chest.

As we start down the hallway to Handy's apartment, a door flies open and a woman almost backs into us. Her voice is thick with scorn. *"Pendejo,"* she says. But before I can see who she's talking to, the door flings shut and she pushes past us, heads for the stairs, sobbing.

Next to Handy's open doorway, a girl, about four years old, is kicking the wall. She has already knocked out a nice toehold. Another few kicks and she'll be down to the lath. Bits of plaster lie at her feet. The end of her patent-leather shoe is white with dust. She kicks steadily, rhythmically. Her mother stands watching, heavy brown arms across her chest. She shakes her head slowly but does nothing. The girl flashes her a quick, searing look.

Behind them an old man with bandaged hands tries to roll a cigarette, spills tobacco, sighs, tries again.

Behind him, two teenaged girls whisper to each other, smiling slyly. Their teased hair touches when they lean close. They're wearing black tank tops and the same shade of purple lipstick. One of the girls tears a twist of beef jerky in half and they hold the pieces like cigarettes, blowing imaginary smoke at the old man.

"What do these people want with your mother?" I whisper to Handy. "They're lined up out here like she's the Pope."

"She's better than the Pope," Handy says. "She's a *bruja*."

"A witch," Mercer says. "She's into healing."

The air out here is suffocating, rank as a jungle. Tacked to the doorframe is what looks like a skinny leather tie. But it's not. It's a snakeskin. Across the doorway is a careful scattering of dirt, feathers, old silver coins.

"Her magic circle," Handy says as we step across. And now I see it trails all around the room. "For protection from curses."

Mercer says, "Boys, we're not in Kansas anymore."

Handy's mother is sitting on the end of the bed. She's huge, serene as a stone carving. She's wearing a loose cotton dress the brown of freshly turned earth, the green of wide, wet leaves. And among the leaves a brighter pattern of birds in flight, birds the color of mustard. Her dark eyes glow in her dark face. I wouldn't be surprised to see flames jump from the twisted stumps of her fingers.

"Don't even try to talk to her," Handy says. He sings the words, as if they're meant for her, as if he's glad to see her. "She doesn't speak English," he sings. "She can't understand a word we say, can you, old buffalo?" She nods, smiles.

"Teach me a word," I ask him. He gives me a look, like I'm kidding him. I pull him aside, make him whisper the word to me so it will seem more like mine when she hears it. His breath is warm against my ear. Mercer's eyes go cold.

"Encantado," I say, taking her hand and bowing my head slightly. Enchanted. She smiles, dips her head.

Then Mercer edges between us and takes her hand, patting it like he's trying to find a vein. "Sudsy huskies, little mother," he says, "sudsy, sudsy huskies." She smiles again and dips her head, fanning herself with a Museum of Natural History brochure, a young girl receiving callers. I feel like pushing Mercer out a window.

There isn't much furniture — a small white sofa, a stuffed chair the color of cocoa, a fold-out canvas cot leaning against the closet door. Edged into a corner is the kitchen, pots simmering on every burner of the stove, a column of steam standing over each. Bowls of beans, rice, and roasted peppers, platters of chicken, beef, fried plantains, and other vegetables, cover the counter. It must be ninety degrees in here. The apartment's two narrow windows are wide open and the blinds rattle lightly, but the breeze dies before it can cross the room.

We drink red wine from bottles without labels. We eat. We drink more wine. Handy's mother does not eat. She drinks rum. On the floor next to her feet is a glass Handy is careful to keep full. Another glass of rum stands on the floor near the edge of the circle, next to a dog-eared picture of Jesus, two candles, and a white plate full of rocks and sea-shells. A thin ribbon of smoke rises from a tray of incense. "*Copal* for the god," Handy explains.

She watches us, her son's friends. We talk. Most of the time Handy doesn't bother to translate our conversation for her. We talk about work, friends, about things that have happened and things we'd like to happen. She sits at the center of it all, peaceful, watching.

Handy shows us his clothes. He's a runner for the Ex-change, where they won't let him wear what he likes: army fatigues streaked with bright pink paint, a slick gray jump-suit, an embroidered djellaba. He's always on the edge of being fired. "For good taste," he says. "They'll fire me for my good taste." We drink more wine. Then Mercer recites a list of people he would pay someone to kill. Stephen, the guy we met in the bar, is third on the list. In the distance I hear glass breaking, engines ripping up the dark, and once a scream and laughter. The only sound from the hall is the girl's kicking, which never stops.

When Handy's mother speaks, her words come from far back in her throat. *"Ale,"* she says.

Handy makes a face but gets up and goes to the door, motioning the woman and child inside. The woman's face is earnest, frightened, full of purpose. The girl has to be pushed ahead of her. When they're close enough, Handy's mother touches the girl's cheek, but the girl twists away. Her mother calmly slaps her, turns her to the old woman, holds her tightly by the chin. The girl trembles with rage. Handy's mother takes something out of her mouth, a soft brown lump she's been chewing. Before the girl knows what's happening, the old woman pushes it into her mouth, tips her small head back, fills the mouth with what might be water. The girl coughs but swallows most of it. Then she yanks away so violently that she falls on the floor. She slaps at her tongue with the palms of her hands. She spits. Her mother quickly drags her to her feet and backs out of the room, thanking the old woman.

Handy comes up behind Mercer's chair and starts to massage his shoulders. Mercer rolls his head lazily from side to side. His voice is sleepy. "We're lucky she didn't bring any animals with her. Her house is full of things in cages."

"Iguanas," Handy says. "Geckos — all kinds of lizards. A

rooster and lots of chickens. Snakes. A pig. A goat. Doves. It's like a zoo. They're to keep curses away from the family. When she has bad dreams about me, she chews some stinking root for hours and sends it to me. I'm supposed to drink it like tea." He makes a face and shivers, waving his hand toward the garbage. "I throw it away. I tell her, '*Mamita,* everybody in America is safe.'"

The old man with bandaged hands comes in. "Get this, get this," Mercer says. He's pointing at the green plaid slacks, the gold shirt with blue piping. He hisses, "Campesino chic."

The old man holds his hands out to her. His voice is low. Slowly she unwraps the bandages, speaking quietly all the time, until the man's swollen, blistered hands are bare. She touches them gently, says some words. She points to a shabby "I Love New York" shopping bag standing in the corner, and Handy digs through it until he finds what she wants, a baby-food jar filled with something like old motor oil. She fingers some of it out of the jar and smooths it carefully over the man's hands, talking all the time. I sit there dazed in the murmur of a language I can't understand. I watch. She rewraps the hands in the bandages. Before he leaves, the old man makes an elaborate farewell in Spanish. He touches his cracked lips to her hand.

I'm expecting the teenagers next, but a guy in a torn T-shirt and jeans crusty with dirt walks in, fear bouncing around in his brown eyes. The air is charged with need. He walks straight to her and drops to his knees with a sharp crack. He can hardly breathe. His words catch in his throat. She touches the top of his head, nods. He gets up quickly and leaves.

I say to Handy, "What is it she does for these people?"

Handy shrugs. "Different things. There are angels of darkness and angels of light. She makes peace with the dark angels."

"However," Mercer says, raising his finger, "they'll never develop fashion sense. Not even magic can. . . ."

But I'm not listening. When I tried to take Cary to the hospital, she was afraid to let me untie her, afraid to let me take her out to the car. "I'll fly away and you'll never find me," she said. When I bent down to untie her ankle, she pulled my hair, punched me, clawed at me. I had to call an ambulance. I stood in the corner while two men fought her into a straitjacket and strapped her to a gurney and rolled her away.

Handy's talking. He says, "One time she told me I should stay away from a blond guy with a scar on his leg. She called me from Mexico just to warn me. That night I met him in a bar. He had the scar, right where she said it would be. He beat me up. He hurt me real good."

"Get her to dream about the market," Mercer says. He's slumped in the chair, his eyes closed. His arms hang limply over the sides. "Then you'll really have something."

The guy in the T-shirt is back, this time with a woman carrying a baby wrapped in a blue blanket. He urges them into the room, toward the old woman, who smiles, makes a cradle of her arms. When the woman hands the baby to her, the blanket slips down. The baby's face is slick and red. The baby is too exhausted to cry, too sick. Its eyes shine with fever.

Handy's mother leans over the baby and coos. With her free hand, she reaches under the bed and brings out a bowl of eggs in water. She sets it on the bed beside her and crushes one of them in her hand, smearing some of the yolk on the baby's forehead. She draws a circle in it with her thumb, whispering. A drop runs into the corner of its eye, but the baby only looks startled and curious. When the old woman hands the baby back to its parents, they hurry from the room, looking relieved and grateful.

Handy brings her a paper towel, and she says something to him. "My mother is tired now," he says. "She'd like to say good night. But before you go she wants you to try something."

When she stands up, I'm as stunned as if a wall of the apartment has fallen away. She is immense. She stands in painful stages. She uproots herself. She walks to the kitchen, slowly rocking forward on the ancient machinery of her hips. She goes to the stove and fills a platter with something from a skillet and brings it over to us, to me.

Handy is excited. "Have you ever eaten blood sausage? It's very good. Eat. My mother will be hurt if you don't like it." She holds the platter under my face. It looks like a plate of scraped knees.

"I hope it tastes better than it looks," I say, and eat a piece. It's gummy and full of gristle. I smile nervously and eat another piece. The old woman smiles. Mercer and Handy smile. I take a big slug of wine to drown the taste, coughing. By now we're all laughing.

The old woman motions to Handy and whispers something to him. He whispers back. She stares at me as she listens, her lips working silently. She has him say it again. He looks bored, impatient. I can hardly breathe. She steps close to me and pats my chest lightly with the palms of her hands. On the web of each hand is a tattoo, a tiny red star. Slowly, carefully, she says, "My son has good friends." She looks at her son, who nods, then looks back at me. Faster now, more confident, she says, "My son has good friends."

As we leave the building, another shower ends. Handy's walking us back to the car. Right away he and Mercer fall behind, leaning against each other, whispering. I want to be by myself anyway. They're half a block behind, but they might as well be at the other end of the universe.

It's quiet. There's no sign of the bikers, only the sharp insinuating smell of oil. A few apartment windows shimmer with blue television light. Somewhere beyond the rooftops the city lights still burn, traffic growls, and far away a siren whines.

Up ahead, the sidewalk is crowded with greasy bags of ripe garbage, chicken bones and fruit rinds trailing out of the splits in their sides. I'm just coming to them when a light flashes from the alley beyond, an engine rumbles.

Behind me, Handy says, "Oh, crud."

And then he's there, a biker slowly rolling his motorcycle out onto the sidewalk. He steers around the heaped-up garbage, keeps coming. As he gets closer, he knocks the

throttle down and duck-walks his bike right up to me. He's
big. He's wearing a faded denim jacket over an orange Harley
T-shirt. His hair is red, what's left of it. His beard is bare in
places. He sits there for a second — his eyes dead, the engine
throbbing under him. Then, at the same time, he wrenches
the throttle and grabs the brake. The bike bucks forward two
or three inches. He does it again and the bike bucks closer.
Once more and he'll drive the front tire between my knees.
Behind me everything is silent.

"Ludes?" he says. Pale blue exhaust gushes softly around
my feet. He shifts his weight, teasing the throttle. "Black
hash? Thai stick? Mushrooms? Grass?"

I don't know if he's asking or offering. I just stand there,
too scared to speak.

"Nothing?" he says, wrenching the throttle.

The love speed. I can feel it through the front of my shirt
pocket like an extra nipple. I dig it out and show him.

"Looks like lunch to me," he says and pushes out his
tongue.

I lean over the front of his bike and place the tab on his
gray tongue. He draws it in, swallows, smiles.

"Much obliged," he says. He walks the bike backward a
few feet and guns the engine. The sidewalk shudders. The
engine thunders, howls, and then he's gone. In seconds he's
nothing but a quiet rattle in the distance.

I feel blessed. I've tasted blood on a back street, and the
whole supernatural world is on my side. I start to walk down
the wet black sidewalk. Now, I think, no one will die. Not
from osteogenic sarcoma or leukoplakia. I'm walking faster

now, running. Not from toxoplasmosis or peripheral neuropathy. Now no one will drift away with dark angels. I'll put my hands inside her tangled hair. I'll hold her head and kiss the vein throbbing at her temple. I'll look into her wild eyes and say, "Here I am, sweetie. Grab hold."

Blues for Marie

ONE AFTERNOON MY MOTHER WALKED OUT our front
door into the hard glare of a Kentucky summer day. She was
carrying an armload of clothes — a few carefully folded
blouses and skirts and a big wad of my clothes, stuff from my
drawer and dirty stuff from the hamper. I had my bike set
upside down in the front yard to see how fast I could crank
the wheel. Would I break the speed of sound? Would I break
the bicycle? It was 1963, I was eleven, still dumb enough to
think I could work my will on the world.

She walked right past me, my socks and underwear
peeling off the pile.

"Hey!"

She walked straight to the curb and shoved the clothes
through the back window of our big blue Fairlane. She went
around to the street side of the car and climbed behind the
wheel. When she had the car running, she leaned over and
popped the passenger door.

"It's now or never, Martin," she called to me.

"What?" I said. "Is the washer broken?"

"You heard me."

I got in beside her and hauled the door shut, thinking we were going to Launderland, that maybe she would give me money for candy and pop.

She pulled away slowly at first, then swung the car in a big U-turn that bucked us up onto the curb and down. When we were back in front of our place but facing the other way, she stopped and stared at the house. I sat there with her, listening to the heavy chug of the engine, looking out at the loose laundry trailing along the sidewalk, at my bicycle, the back wheel still turning, at my father clawing the venetian blinds apart for a better look.

My father was a mystery. He had a way of looking at me that made me feel like something he'd spilled and didn't know how to clean up. But I didn't like sitting in the car, looking at him like that. It made him seem small and pitiful. It made everything look small and pitiful: the white ranch house with its neat border of gravel, the scrawny pear tree in the center of the small patch of burned-out grass, the upside-down bicycle rocking lightly with each wobbly turn of the wheel.

"I guess we can get the socks and stuff later," I said.

Still facing the house, she said, "This is about as late as it gets, kid." She turned to me, her mouth wide and tight. Already I could see the pale blue bruise coloring the left side of her face, spreading under her eye. I couldn't help myself. I reached out to touch her. When she saw my hand coming, she slapped it away.

We drove through flat fields and sad mill towns. At night

we parked on the shoulder and slept in the car. She couldn't have pulled very far off the road, because every car rushing past rocked the Fairlane, high beams blazing. If I held up my hand, light washed slowly up and down my arm.

She stopped only long enough for us to eat.

"When's Dad coming?"

"Yeah, right."

I knew better but I wanted her to talk. She hardly ever did. And then it was usually after we'd finished off a sack of burgers and fries from a dairy bar. "Did you get enough?" Sometimes, when she thought I was asleep, she'd think out loud. "The drinking I could put up with. It wasn't the drinking. And I could live with the hitting."

It was true my father could be rough. But she'd told me herself that he was rough because we mattered so much to him. She didn't have to bother. That's the way I thought fathers were supposed to be.

The day before we left him, I had come home with a bloody nose and a gash under my right eye. My father held my face in his hands and pressed my cut with his thumb until I cried.

"Baby," he said quietly. "You're a baby and a coward, and there's no place in my house for you." He led me to the door and gently pushed me outside, then locked it.

I stood in the yard for a long time, my throat stopped with shame. The wind blew. The sun swung overhead. After what felt like hours, I turned away and walked off down the railroad tracks. I walked for a long time, stepping carefully from tie to tie. The sun was low. I lay down in the weeds to rest. My face was swollen and tender. I was so tired. I fell asleep listening to kids being called to supper.

Someone was shaking my shoulder. "Get up. Get up." It was my mother, bending over me in the fading light. "Get up." She walked me across the field and down the tracks for a good half mile. Below the hem of her dress her legs were scratched and bleeding.

The next day, on the road, she'd gaze into the rearview as if we were being followed. Sometimes she'd pull off the road and wait while cars passed. She'd climb out and stare down the road behind us, almost disappointed. Then she'd settle behind the wheel again, always with a look at me like I was a hitchhiker she regretted stopping for.

After two days on the road, long enough for me to like the highway life, we came to a coal town in northeastern Pennsylvania. I never knew why we stopped there. Maybe that's where the money ran out. Maybe my mother saw a sign of hope in the sooty foothills and sulfurous air of anthracite country.

Esther, Pennsylvania, was a town full of old men, mostly retired miners. The coal had petered out long ago, leaving nothing but loose heaps of culm and mine fires in the hills. The old men sat on their porches, coughing up their lungs, mumbling to themselves, screaming at you in Polish and Russian.

We moved into one side of a double-block in a run-down neighborhood near the railroad tracks. We covered the broken windows with newspaper and wondered what to do about the dead Buick the former tenant had left in the front yard. The next day, my mother found a job at J & W Sportswear, sewing slacks at piece rate for Jimmy and Wes, the brothers who owned the place. And the day after that, our car died its last death, so she walked the three miles to and from work every day.

On the other side of our double-block lived Stanko Sawicki. The kids called him "Stinko" because of the medicine smell that clung to him, though I don't know how they got close enough for a whiff. In the evenings he liked to sit out on the front porch and threaten his neighbors. When he was healthier, they said, he used to throw rocks at them. Now that his lungs were shot, he just waved a stick weakly as they passed, but it was enough to scare them. Little kids crossed the street instead of walking in front of his house. Women hurried by with their bags of groceries. Even Bootsie, the neighborhood dog, stopped at the end of Sawicki's sidewalk and wouldn't pass until the old man went in.

At first I liked to sit on the porch, listening to my transistor. But pretty soon I'd hear Sawicki fumbling at his doorknob. I'd slip inside our house and watch him from behind the curtain. He was easy to avoid. Because of the black lung, he moved pretty slow. He had to wear an oxygen mask all the time, a big green plastic thing that looked like an athletic cup. He carried a long coil of clear tubing that trailed from the mask to the oxygen tank inside his house. At night I could hear the tank through the wall, chuffing like a locomotive. The tube was long enough to let him roam his property but played out somewhere near the front sidewalk, like a leash. But he was still scary. With his mask on he was the Creature from the Black Lagoon, out of his element on land but no less dangerous.

It was hard for me to make friends in Esther. School was almost over for the year. Everybody there already had friends, and there were no kids my age in my neighborhood. I didn't mind. I was tired of being teased for my hillbilly accent. I said "*cee*ment" for "cement," "*zee*ro" for "zero," and "orl" for "oil." They made me afraid to open my mouth. A friend would've just meant ridicule on a regular basis.

Still, I hung around them when I could. I was afraid to be by myself, afraid my father might fly out of the shadows to punish me for ruining all our lives.

On Saturday mornings — while my mother slept late, took long baths, and did her hair — I'd go out front with my transistor and deck of cards. I'd taken to sitting behind the wheel of the rusted-out Buick, where I'd prop the radio on the dash and tune in some songs. It didn't bother me that the Buick had no tires and was buried up to its axles. Or that it smelled like cats, or that the floor was littered with empty beer bottles. Sawicki couldn't reach me there.

I loved music. The stations you could get in Esther mostly played polkas or "Swap Shop," but sometimes I got lucky. The Everly Brothers, Buddy Holly, Carl Perkins. I pretended the music was mine, that it existed only for me.

When Clarence drove up in his green pickup that first Saturday, I was listening to Pat Boone and dealing a hand to an imaginary friend. I liked the slap and whisper of the cards.

"That ain't real music you're listening to." The voice startled me, so close and loud. There was his big black face gazing in at my window. Clarence was the assistant to Dr. Kern, the veterinarian down the street. Once a week he came by collecting old newspapers to use in the kennel.

"And what the hell kind of card game is that?" He pointed his chin at the mess of cards I'd spread next to me, some of them sliding onto the floor or into the seat crack. I didn't know what to say. He went around the other side of the car and climbed in.

He gathered up the cards, made a face at the radio, and said, "You like Mr. Pat Boone singing 'Tutti Frutti'?"

"Sure," I told him. "I like it fine." Clarence had close-cropped hair and a big, friendly face. He had a way of looking past you when he talked, then all at once zeroing in when he wanted to make a point.

"Well, I'm here to tell you that ain't the real 'Tutti Frutti.' " He swung his gaze at me. "That's 'Tutti Frutti' in a monkey suit. You want to hear real 'Tutti Frutti,' you come by my place some time. Now let's see if you know how to shuffle those cards."

Until school let out for the year, I did nothing but wait from one week to the next for Clarence's visits.

He taught me things. How to shuffle. How to play rummy. Then blackjack and several kinds of poker. He told me about Chicago, where he grew up, about playing his saxophone in all-night jazz clubs and smoking reefer. How his best friend stole his limo service right out from under him. He told me about the Roman Empire, where he'd been a general in Caesar's army. And about Africa, where he'd been a tribal king, according to the Gypsies. He gave me my secret name, Marcus, and taught me to deal off the bottom, a trick I was to use only if the other guy was cheating, which I could count on fairly often. He knew how to talk to an eleven-year-old boy. He knew the things I needed to know. When he described the world, it didn't seem like a place dead set against me but seemed a place full of secrets and possibilities.

Sometimes, before my mother came out, he'd give me advice, though I never quite understood any of it. He'd tell me about an alley fight or somebody's wife he stole, and finish by saying, "I'll say this for myself, though: I've never been one of those B-flat kind of guys." And he'd fix me with those red-rimmed eyes so that all I could do was nod.

The only wife he ever talked about was his first, Darla. He said her name as if she were a picture he'd seen once in a museum.

"There was a woman," he'd sigh. "I never should have run around on that little bit. It's drink that did me in. Drinking throws you down the slippery slope. And then the gonads raise their ugly heads and finish you off."

Most Saturdays, my mother just left the newspapers on the front porch for him, like all our neighbors. But one day she came right out to the car and opened my door. She stood there just watching us. Finally she said, "What's all this about?"

"We're just visiting," I said.

Clarence looked up, smiling, and did his best trick, a shuffle that ended with the cards cascading from one hand to the other.

My mother pinched her mouth at him, but it was plain that she was pleased. She leaned into the open door in a way that embarrassed me. "Don't you go teaching my boy a lot of flim-flam."

"No, ma'am, not me."

She had trouble meeting people. My friends' pa[...]
called her "the divorcée," like she was some exotic dis[...]
There was no fancy word for what I was, but it was s[...]
thing close to "bastard."

I remember the day we left my father, how we sat i[...]
car and watched him watching us. Maybe she was wond[...]
whether anything would ever be the same, and whethe[...]
was good or bad. And here was Clarence, the first fri[...]
person she'd met in Esther, with his good looks an[...]
generous smile. How else could things have gone?

After that first day, she came out every Saturday wit[...]
drinks and sandwiches. Her visits got longer and lon[...]
didn't want her there. Clarence was *my* friend. We had t[...]
to talk about that she wouldn't understand. All sh[...]
wanted to talk about was the weather, dog personalitie[...]
is your drink cold enough?

One Saturday he told us how he got his nickname[...]

"We were doing a little thing at a club called The I[...]
This woman kept coming around. She was interes[...]
musicians, especially sax players, who had a rep for m[...]
more than music." He smiled nervously at my m[...]
standing like always in the open door. When she didn't[...]
he kept talking. "Wasn't any truth to it, but there you g[...]
kept calling me 'honey' this and 'honey' that. My ban[...]
were all good little players, but they were full of[...]
Everybody but me had a nickname back then — 'Big [...]
'White Bear,' 'Mr. Dirty,' you know. Pretty soon[...]
going, 'Nice solo, honey' and 'Pick it up at the eigh[...]

honey.' Before long, the name turned into 'Honeyman.' And then, after my third marriage went bad, 'Honeymoon.' "

"What happened to the band?" my mother asked.

"Killed is what. One by one. First our drummer, from an overdose. Then somebody got a disease. Rock 'n' roll did in the rest of us. I see them once in a while. But we don't hang out. We don't even go by our nicknames anymore. Now we're just ourselves."

"Look," I said, arching the deck in my hands so it fluttered like a trapped bird.

By July my mother was inviting him into the house for a cold drink almost as soon as he climbed into the Buick. If I wanted time with him, I'd have to do it some other way. He lived in a one-room cinder-block cottage behind Dr. Kern's office, close to the animals. One night, after supper, I went over there, making my way carefully down the walk between the cages. Dogs began to tear at the gates, barking and howling. Cats pressed themselves into the corners and yowled. I held my hands over my ears and ran for Clarence's door.

"Those animals are sounding especially damned hell-acious," he said as he let me in, not at all surprised to see me. He sat me down in his living room with a soda, poured himself a glass of whiskey, and turned on his hi-fi.

The first singer he played was Fats Domino — "Ah found mah three-ill own Blue-berry Heel." That voice so full of sex and sadness — things I wouldn't understand until years later. I wanted more. He played me the real "Tutti Frutti." Little Richard's falsetto made my neck hairs stand

straight out. But most of all he liked the blues. He had
hundreds of 45s. He played Eddie Squareface Samuel singing
"Shake Me, Thrill Me." He played Bad Allen Boudreaux's
"Bust Loose Blues."

Maybe it was the place or the sip of whiskey that burned
a searing path down my throat, but the music made me wild.
It blew through me like I was a big, empty room. "Aw," I said.
"Aw."

"Is that music?" he said, slapping the arm of his chair. "Is
that some damn music?"

He showed me old handbills from his days playing saxophone in Chicago clubs. He showed me pictures of his
younger self standing next to fat black men with worn-out
faces and shiny horns tucked under their arms. "That was a
thousand years ago," he said.

I was this eleven-year-old white kid in Pennsylvania, this
virgin, a sixth grader afraid to change into his gym clothes in
front of other boys. But that night I was a black blues singer,
a man full of sexual woe, a man who drank too much and
blamed his gonads for love gone and love gone wrong. Never
mind that I didn't know gonads from Grapette. The next few
days were just dead time until I could go back for more.

By the end of summer I knew some things. About music.
About cards. About sex. I knew that a full house beats a
straight every damn day of the week. I knew that women are
as dangerous as plutonium. I knew that some guys hurt Buck
Clayton, screwing up his lip for life. And that Pops was a man
who was never too big to play out. I knew that the best song

in the world was "Green Dolphin Street," because of its freaky chord changes. I had no idea who these people were or what Clarence was talking about, but it mattered to me. Barrelhouse and boogie piano, the sad wail of saxophones, the sweet heartache of the blues.

By the time school started, I was living and breathing his secret world. I wasn't the goofy hillbilly kid afraid to open his mouth. I was changed. I affected a weary swagger. I dragged my voice an octave lower, losing the ends of my sentences in the stony silence of my memories. I wore shades day and night and made myself wait a full ten-count before answering any of my teachers' questions. Everybody back off, I was saying. This man is burning with the blues. With money from odd jobs, I bought a threadbare black suit from Goodwill and wore it every day. In my mind I looked just like those old men in the pictures.

Clarence had lost his saxophone in a poker game a long time ago, but he gave me his old strap, which I wore like a tie. Kids — the same ones who used to make fun of my accent — started asking me to do stuff with them after school. But I'd hook my thumb in the strap and shake my head slowly. "I got to put the iron to my lips, man." I'd leave them staring after me, their mouths hanging open. I was a blues man. I was turning black before their very eyes. Everything about me was a message. You think you know me, but you do not. You do not.

Early in the school year, Clarence came by with a one-watt radio transmitter, his hi-fi, and a big box of records. He made me a deal. He'd give me a dollar a week if I'd broadcast the blues every Saturday afternoon while he had lunch with my mother.

We set it up in the empty garage behind my house, spreading a threadbare Persian rug and pushing an old stuffed chair in front of the upturned apple crate that held the equipment. He arranged his gilded wire racks of records all around the chair.

I sat down and flipped the toggle on the gray steel face of the transmitter. He said he'd picked the thing out of the trash behind one of the big houses. When I laid my hand on the box, I could feel the tubes warming up. I could hear dust sizzling inside. The air began to hum. I cleared my throat and pushed the red button on the base of the microphone.

"This is Mad Marcus," I said, my words squawking from the transistor we'd set on the oil drum against the wall. Every sound in the room came to life — the squeaky springs in the cushion under me, my elbow propped on the table, every breath I took. I lowered my voice. "This is Mad Marcus, and I'm here to bring you the blues."

At first the signal reached no farther than the other side of the garage. No wonder somebody'd thrown the transmitter away. But when we hooked up the antenna to the wall of chicken wire separating the two stalls, Clarence heard me loud and clear all the way out to the street and all the way down the block.

In the middle of Arthur Somerville's piano solo on "Cry Cry Blues," Stanko Sawicki showed up at the garage door. He was not happy. He slapped at the glass with his coiled tubing, the sound of small bones tumbling together. It turned out that my signal was so strong it blotted out every other signal on his radio.

He liked to spend his Saturdays listening to a little Mantovani, a little Skitch Henderson, some Andy Williams. I'd hear it through the wall. What I gave him was Wild Willie Dupree singing "Black Bottom Blues" and Meat Jackson doing "Sally in the Alley" and Lips LeGrange doing "Empty Bottle, Empty Bed."

And Sawicki would be at the door, rattling the knob, wheezing, "What kind of ... Halloween getup ... and what the hell ... kind of music. ... ?"

"If you have to ask," I said, quoting Pops, "you'll never know."

Part of me hoped that the music, through some miracle of electronics, would reach my father all the way back in Kentucky, and that he would hear how things were different now, how the music could make us all new and good.

I was out there every Saturday, playing my music. Nothing stopped me. Not Sawicki's threats to call the police. Nothing. I sat hunched over my microphone, spinning the blues, talking the blues. I was Mad Marcus, and I was too cool to care.

One day in early November, my mother called in sick. I knew it was a lie because she started doing her hair like she was going out. I begged her to let me stay home, too. I had a sore throat, I said, which was true, but I also had a civics test I hadn't studied for. It was gray and cold out, so I was bored after five minutes of freedom. That's why I thought it was a miracle when Clarence showed up. My mother and I both met him at the door. I remember the confused look on his face, though I didn't pay any attention to it at the time.

"How'd you know we were home?" I said. "This is great. I'll play some tunes." And even though I was sick, my mother let me go out to the garage.

I flipped on the space heater and warmed up the transmitter. I turned on my transistor radio. Sometimes, when I was feeling ambitious, I included a newscast in the Blues Revue, holding the transistor to the microphone while the announcer ran through the top stories, then yanking it away before the station ID. I set the transistor on the oil drum, the volume low. I worked out my playlist and started the show with my theme song, Duke's "It Don't Mean a Thing if It Ain't Got That Swing." It wasn't exactly the blues, but it was from one of Clarence's old 78s, and I knew he liked Ben Webster's solo.

Things went well for a while. I played all Clarence's favorites. I pictured him telling my mother the kinds of stories he told me, about playing at places with names like Lockhart's and the Peek-a-Boo Lounge and the Club Sudan.

My favorite story was about how he played with Coltrane once. I made him tell it over and over.

"I used to listen at the band out back of this little club," he'd say, "through the kitchen door. One time I heard Trane." He'd shake his head, remembering. "This was before Miles. Hell, it was before Trane. He burned that place down. Him and that big fat tenor. I waited for him after. When he came out, I got up the nerve to say, 'Mr. Coltrane, I want to cap a few tunes with you.' Without batting an eye, he took me to his hotel. And I was not half bad. In those days, I had fast ears and hungry hands. I pushed back the walls a little. But when it got down to doing the do, well, let's just say I got my hair cut real close."

I heard Sawicki before I saw him, his dry torn breaths. This time he was inside the garage — I'd forgotten to lock the door — just a few feet away, his oxygen tube stretched taut to the door.

My song was ending. I leaned over the microphone. In my lowest, quietest voice, I said, "Mr. Five by Five, Jimmy Rushing, shoutin' and swingin' 'Sent for You Yesterday.' " I had the next record on now and focused all my attention on the microphone. I pretended I was whispering into someone's ear, telling secrets. "Let's stay in this R and B groove a little longer. Here's Sugar Pie DeSanto's 'I Want to Know,' the song that's taking her all over the chitlin circuit." At the instant I finished talking, Sugar Pie hit her first loud mournful note. I was good.

Sawicki dropped the green mask on the floor and took three faltering steps toward me. He was a tall man, with a pale face and dark, sagging eyelids. His hands looked blue, and the skin was as loose as a pair of work gloves. He was like Frankenstein's monster ripping loose from his IVs and umbilicals. He spoke in a rough whisper. It scared me more than if he'd yelled something.

"That spade . . . poking . . . your old lady again?"

My face burned.

I stood up and stepped out from behind the microphone. I walked up to him as close as I dared and faced him in my black suit, my black pointed shoes, my black shades. I thought my look alone was enough to send him running, but it didn't work.

His words, when they came, were carried on a dry croak. "Your father like . . . his wife . . . whoring around . . . to that jigaboo music?"

My eyes stung. "You —"

"Come . . . ," he said, pointing at his mask. "I want . . . to show you . . . something."

I didn't want to go. I didn't want to do anything he asked. But when I picked up the mask and gave it to him — I didn't want him dying on me — an agreement was sealed.

It took him forever to lead me back to his side of the house. He moved with slow, faltering steps. Because he had to hold the oxygen mask to his face, I walked ahead, gathering the loose tubing as we got close to the house.

At the back door he stopped, to catch his breath, I thought. When he shot a quick mean glare at me, I knew I was supposed to open the door. It was heavy and so thick with old paint that it made a shredding sound when I pushed it open, as if I had torn away a piece of the wall.

I'd never been in a stranger's house before, not by myself. I knew I wasn't supposed to talk to strangers, let alone go into their houses. And I was worried that my record might end before I got back. But I couldn't help it. I went in.

The kitchen smelled faintly sour. There was a cat on the

counter, tearing at the side of a bread bag. When it saw us, it showed its teeth and hissed. The old man shambled past me, paying no attention, and led me into the dining room.

There was a hospital bed with rails in there, butted right up against the mahogany sideboard. Standing in a hand truck was a tall oxygen tank that looked dangerous as a torpedo. Next to it was a blue metal box with a gauge on top and a small black bellows pumping inside a glass jar.

"Upstairs," he wheezed, his voice hollow in the plastic mask, "if you want . . . to see." I'd heard about old men who liked to touch kids, and I wasn't going to have any part of this, but he took the tubing from me and said, "Go on!" It was clear he wasn't coming with me.

Each step gave out a sharp ache as I climbed. At the top I turned to look at the old man smiling monstrously up at me. He crooked his thumb over his shoulder. He wanted me in the front bedroom. I was happy to go, happy to be out of his sight.

The bed was large and covered with a faded white chenille spread, a partly unraveled braided rug at its foot. At first I didn't pay much attention to the hole in the wall. Someone — I couldn't imagine Sawicki finding the strength — had hacked away at the plaster, making a ragged opening the size of a football. Was this what he wanted me to see? I dragged a wooden chair to the wall and stepped up on it. Whoever had chopped the hole had also worked a tiny slit in the plaster on the other side, our side. I leaned closer. A dribble of light came through. Closer, half my face in the hole. The air inside smelled dry and poisonous, air from a tomb. I could hear music coming through the wall. I pressed my eye to the slit. It was hard to see anything, and when I did, I jerked my head back, nearly falling off the chair.

I ran downstairs. The old man was too excited to speak. He kept sucking at his mask. I grabbed the big tank of oxygen and pushed at it with all my strength, but the hand truck only rolled a few inches.

He shook his coiled tubing at me. "Did ... you?" I backed away from him, into the kitchen. The cat yowled. The old man followed, slapping my chest with the tubing. "What do you think ... now?" He backed me against the table.

I pushed him. I laid my hands on his chest and I shoved. But he just stood there, a dry laugh clicking at the back of his throat.

I couldn't help myself. I grabbed a butter knife, took up the tubing, and cut through a loop of it.

He stumbled back, trailing ten feet of loose tubing, his eyes rolling wildly. I threw the knife on the floor, backing away.

"You!" I yelled so loud the cat flew off the counter and ran for the cellar door. "You wouldn't know a flat five from a sharp nine!" When I left he was hugging the tank, jamming the end of the tube onto its steel nipple.

Back in the garage, I tore off my jacket and threw it at the chicken wire. I flung my sax strap into the rafters. I took my shades off and snapped them in half.

When my eye had adjusted to the slit, I thought my mother was hurt. Clarence was leaning her slowly back onto the bed, as if she were in too much pain to lie down by herself. And her whole body seemed to be wrapped in bandages. I nearly cried out. Then he rolled her over and undid her brassiere. My face burned. I felt like a fool.

And to make matters worse, they didn't have the clock radio tuned to my music. They were listening to Harry James, the trumpet player on the Kleenex commercial.

I peeled the record off the turntable and ran outside to the front of the house. I flung it at the bedroom window as hard as I could and watched it glance off and skitter across the gritty porch roof. I ran back to the garage and brought out a full rack of records, ready to sail them at the window one by one, until they were lying all over — on the porch roof, in the yard, wedged in the bushes, shattered in the street. But I couldn't. I stood there staring into the black vinyl of the record in my hands until a terrible idea came to me.

Back in the garage, I cued up the record and put on my best blues voice: "This is Mad Marcus, coming at you with a little number for Clarence and his little number, Marie McDaniel." I had never said my mother's name out loud before, and it felt like swearing to say it now. "Clarence and Marie. They're upstairs right now at 98 Clark Street, and they're doing it." I played Big Joe Turner, singing "I Can Tell by the Way You Smell, You Been Doing Something Wrong."

I wanted a horror movie scene, angry villagers converging on the castle. I wanted screaming squad cars, outrage on a grand scale. At the very least, I wanted a mob out front talking in low voices and pointing at the house, at those burning bedroom windows. But I got nothing.

I played Blind Boy Peterson's "Jump Jelly Jump" and

214

Sweet Willie's "Stompin' with Sally" and Alvin Memphis Motherwell's "Hold Tight, All Right."

"Where are those ugly gonads now, Clarence?" I talked myself hoarse. "You hear me, Clarence? You hear me, Ma? I'm playing you every low-down dirty song I know." I played Axel Renfro's "Slip and Slide," Slammin' Sam Cochran's "Sticky Like I Like It," and Tommy "The Juice Man" Jackson's "Work It In."

When the last song ended, the needle drifted toward the label, crackled, then lifted with a pop. But nothing changed. The street was as quiet as before.

"Dad," I said into the microphone, "it's me, Martin. Can you hear me?"

But in the silence, all I heard was the newscaster's voice on my transistor. There was something strange about the way he kept repeating words: "Motorcade . . . three shots . . . Parkland Hospital . . ." and what I heard at first as "one P.M. central *stranded* time."

I slammed through the kitchen and banged up the stairs. I pushed open the bedroom door without knocking, grateful to see my mother in her yellow bathrobe. There was no sign of Clarence, but his clothes lay all over the floor.

I pulled myself up to my full height and said, "The President's been shot! The President is dead, you cruel bitch!" It was a phrase I'd heard my father say, and it was him I was thinking of.

I thought she'd knock my teeth out, but all she said was "Come here, baby." She took my hands and pulled me to her. "Come here."

*   *   *

When we first moved to Esther, I liked to meet her coming home from work. I'd walk halfway and wait. When she came up to me, I'd say, "I thought you might like some company."

"You mean you thought you might con me into a Coke."

"I *am* a little thirsty," I'd say, and if she was in a good mood, we'd stop at a diner she liked. We always sat at the counter because she didn't think she had to leave a tip there.

Sometimes, as we drank our Cokes, she'd hold out a thumb and show me an inflamed red dot in the middle of her nail, and then, turning the thumb over dramatically, another one on the other side, a dried nipple of blood.

"Ran another goddamn needle clear through my goddamn thumb," she'd say. "It's getting so I don't even feel it anymore." She'd close her fingers and thumbs, saying, "The next time you see me, my goddamn fingers will probably be sewn together. Then who's going to buy you Cokes?"

"You," I'd say between sips.

"Oh, sure, me." And she'd try to pick up her change with the ends of her fingers. Coins fell, dancing on the counter, and I'd laugh and spin on my stool, still young enough to love my mother without caring who knew it.

These days I'll see my mother and Clarence coming out of a bar or restaurant, or shopping at the mall. Once I saw them at the Downs, shredding their losing tickets, tossing them in the air and laughing, blind to the ugly space everyone made around them. Sometimes, I think, a person can be a hero without doing anything more than living her life.

Saturdays are mine now. Clarence and I play poker and listen to music. During the good solos we lose track of the game and just sit there with our eyes closed. When we drink too much, we argue a little. About whether Maurice "Sonny" Stitt played more horn than any man alive. "And I'm counting Bird!" Clarence says. About whether this or that tenor solo is by Jimmy Forest or Frank "Floor Show" Culley. Sometimes I'll bring him a new record and he'll wave his hands and yell, "Get that tuneful crap out my face!" Then we laugh at ourselves and drink some more.

Last month I bought him a saxophone from one of the guys at J&W Sportswear, after his kid lost interest. He won't let me listen to him yet. First he wants to get his chops back. He says it's not a pretty sight. Your lips bleed after laying off for that long. I listen anyway, through the window on the alley.

Most days he wears his work clothes, whether he's working or not, but when he practices he wears a white shirt and black pants. He starts by sitting, head down, like he's thinking why go through with this? He leans back, rubbing his fingers across the blue bruise of his mouth, stroking its sides, pulling on his lips.

The sax has pearl buttons. The bell is shiny, but the neck is the glossy yellow of butter gone bad. He used to say the sax is like a strange animal with all its organs growing on the outside, which is a good definition for a lot of things.

Then he has a sip of the whiskey at his elbow, gets up, and stands in the middle of the small room. The sax shines like the gold sash of an African king. He tongues the mouthpiece, then rolls his head back, his eyes gone to white, and blows. For a while the horn won't do what he wants. He plays left, he plays right. The horn flames and fizzles. He wrestles with it. It shrieks and yelps. Then, after a while, something happens. He finds the grain, and suddenly you can feel every breath. It's a sound that burrows into the pit of your stomach and then swims back up to your head, fills it, splits it open, like a headache only good, like a headache you hope will stay with you every day of the world. It's some damn music.